January Joy

Annie Seaton

The Enchanted Village: 2

ISBN 978-1-7644569-2-0

Dedication

Wishing all my dear readers,

Happy New Year.

ironically—had died and left her Hawthorn Cottage. No conditions, no strings. Just a solicitor's letter and a set of keys and the bewildering reality that Joanna now owned a house in a Cotswold village she'd never heard of.

It felt like charity from beyond the grave. As if Victoria had looked at Joanna's life and thought, "My poor cousin woman needs saving."

She must have had ESP.

'It's fine,' Joanna said aloud, just to hear a voice. Her breath fogged white in the air. 'It's absolutely fine.'

It wasn't fine. She was fifty-one years old, standing in a freezing cottage in a village where she knew no one, with three hundred and forty-seven pounds to her name and nowhere else to go.

The thought overwhelmed her; she pushed it away and went looking for the kitchen.

She stepped through a doorway at the back of the sitting room into an old farmhouse kitchen with a deep ceramic sink and an ancient Aga that, when she brushed her fingers along the top, was as cold as stone. A battered wooden table sat beneath a window that looked out onto a snow-covered garden. And there, tucked in the corner where the kitchen met a glass-walled extension she hadn't noticed before, was a door.

Joanna turned the handle and found herself in a small conservatory, barely bigger than a garden shed. It had glass walls, a glass roof, and terracotta tiles on the floor. A single wingback chair was angled toward the windows, ready to catch any winter sun that might sneak through the clouds. The chair's blue fabric was faded but clean, its arms smoothed out from years of use.

Her throat tightened. This was the kind of place someone had loved once. A place where you'd sit with morning tea and watch the garden wake up, where you could finally take a deep breath after days of stress. She backed out quickly and closed the door.

Not expecting to find anything in the cottage, she'd stopped at a Tesco Express on the drive and bought bread, butter, tea, milk, and a few tins of soup, beans, and beef stew. Enough to last a week if she was careful. After that... well. She'd sort something out. She used to be good at sorting things out.

But now? No, not anymore.

For the past ten years, she'd stumbled from one crisis to the next—Mum's diagnosis, Dad's stroke three years later, bills and prescriptions and hospital visits and two exhausting years of round-the-clock care for them both. And before all that...

Marcus.

She closed her eyes and took a deep breath and refused to think about her ex.

After bringing the shopping bags from the car to the kitchen, she set the kettle to boil on the Aga's cold surface, then shook her head as she remembered it wasn't on. She found an electric kettle on the counter instead, filled it and waited for it to heat up.

While the kettle warmed up, she opened cupboards until she found some mugs, and was surprised to find tea bags. It looked like Victoria had left the basics in case she ever took up the offer to stay. The cupboards were lined with old newspaper, dated 2019. Seven years ago. Had the cottage been empty all that time? It was certainly dusty enough.

When the tea was brewed, Joanna wrapped

both hands around the mug, soaking up its warmth. She should unpack, find the airing cupboard, and see if there were any blankets. Work out how to get the heating on, if there was any.

There were a lot of things she should do.

Instead, she walked back to the sitting room and stood by the window, looking out.

The village green was picture-perfect under its layer of snow. A stone cross stood at its centre, worn smooth by centuries. Cottages clustered around the green like gossiping neighbours, lights glowing gold in windows. A pub—The Old Swan, according to its swinging sign—looked cosy and inviting on the far side.

As Joanna watched, a couple walked past the cottage. A tall man with dark hair going silver at the temples, rugged up in a thick coat and scarf. Beside him, a petite woman bundled in a purple coat that was cheerfully at odds with the winter grey. They had their arms linked, heads bent together, talking. The man said something, and the woman laughed, the sound carrying clearly in the cold air.

Suddenly, a wave of loneliness hit Joanna hard, and she had to lean against the window frame to steady herself.

She didn't know them and probably never would. She felt totally out of practice when it came to being around people, especially making the small talk that leads to friendships. A decade of caregiving had drained her of everything she once loved. She had turned invisible while caring for others.

Marcus had left on a Tuesday in March. She remembered because the daffodils were blooming in their garden, bright yellow and unaware of how much her life was about to change. He had sat her down at the kitchen table—their kitchen table, in their house, which she'd spent five years making into a home—and told her he'd been seeing Amanda from the office for eight months. He was leaving. The house was his, and she needed to be out by the end of the month.

'You must have known I wasn't happy,' he'd said, as if that explained everything. As if thirteen years of marriage could be tossed aside because he was bored.

She'd moved in with Mum two weeks later. Mum, who'd just been diagnosed with the illness that took her. Her lovely mother, who'd needed someone to care for her.

Joanna had always been good at being needed until Marcus stopped needing her.

The couple disappeared from view, leaving the green empty again, just snow and shadows and an aura of loneliness.

Joanna turned away from the window. Okay, time to unpack. That's what she'd do. Her fingers were numb around the mug. The tea had gone cold already, a scum forming on its surface.

The sitting room was so cold she could see her breath.

Why didn't I ask the solicitor about heating? Why didn't I—

Suddenly, the fireplace roared to life.

Joanna dropped her mug. It shattered on the flagstones, tea spreading in a dark puddle. She stumbled back, hitting the edge of a dust-sheeted sofa, and caught herself before she fell into the dusty depths of the cover.

The fire burned cheerfully in the grate with actual flames in orange and gold, crackling around logs that she definitely hadn't put there because there hadn't been any logs and she hadn't lit anything and—

'No.' Her voice came out high and shaking. 'No, that's not... that didn't...'

The fire crackled. Heat began to fill the room, pushing back the cold.

Joanna's heart raced. She was going mad. That was the only explanation. The stress of the last decade had finally cracked something inside her, and now she was standing in a freezing cottage, seeing fires that didn't exist.

She should leave. Get back in her car and drive to... where? She had nowhere else to go.

But the fire kept burning. Real heat. Actual warmth that reached into her cold bones and whispered, you're safe here.

Slowly, carefully, she edged closer. The flames danced, orange and gold and hypnotic. She held out her shaking hands and felt warmth soak into her frozen fingers. For the first time since arriving, she could feel her toes.

It was real.

'I'm going mad,' she whispered. But the fire crackled cheerfully, like it was saying, does it matter?

The fire popped, sending up a shower of sparks, and she jumped back.

For a moment, Joanna stood in the middle of

the sitting room, surrounded by dust-sheeted furniture and broken crockery, warming herself by the strange fire. Then she walked very carefully to the front door, picked up her suitcase, and took it upstairs.

She'd deal with everything tomorrow. The fire, the craziness of it all, the fact that her mind was clearly breaking due to being overtired and stressed—she'd deal with all of it tomorrow. She'd wake up to the cold light of day and get this cottage organised.

The bedroom at the front of the cottage was small and cold, but the bed was made up with clean sheets, at least. She ran her fingers over the soft cotton, checking it wasn't damp and then lay down fully clothed, and pulled a thin blanket over herself. Through the window, she could see snow beginning to fall again, soft and gentle, wrapping the cottage in a cosy layer.

She closed her eyes. Downstairs, the fire crackled and burned. Warming an empty cottage for a woman with nowhere else to go.

Tomorrow, Joanna told herself. Tomorrow, she'd work out what was wrong with her. She would pull herself together and make the most of staying in the cottage.

Tomorrow, she'd work out what to do next. *Tomorrow.*

But for now, she would welcome sleep and not think the ways she'd failed—as a wife, as a daughter, as a woman who should have built some kind of secure life for herself.

Outside, the snow kept falling.

Downstairs, the fire kept burning.

And Joanna lay in the dark of Hawthorn Cottage, in a village full of strangers, wondering if she'd be happy again.

Chapter Two

Joanna woke to daylight and birdsong and the lingering smell of woodsmoke. For a moment, she lay still, disoriented, before everything came rushing back. The cottage. The fire that had lit itself. The feeling that she might be losing it.

She sat up slowly. Her body ached from sleeping in her clothes, and her mouth tasted sour. The bedroom was freezing again, her breath misting in the air.

Downstairs, she could hear the faint crackle of flames.

'Right,' she said to the empty room. 'Right.'

She went downstairs in yesterday's clothes, her hair was a mess, and she didn't care. The fire was still burning in the sitting room grate; logs reduced to glowing embers but still giving off heat. As she stood there staring at it, a log shifted and settled, sending up sparks.

Real. It was still real.

Joanna shook her head, took a step back and

then went to make a cup of tea.

The kitchen was a bit warmer than upstairs, though not by much. She filled the electric kettle, set it to boil, and opened a can of baked beans with shaking hands. She ate them cold, standing at the counter, because she couldn't work out how to light the Aga and didn't trust anything in this cottage to behave normally anyway. What she wouldn't give for a thick slice of toast.

The beans tasted of tin and salt and nothing else. She forced down half of it and put the rest in the fridge that hummed quietly in the corner. At least that worked like it was supposed to.

She made tea and wrapped her hands around another mug, even though they weren't cold anymore. The fire had warmed the downstairs enough that she could feel her fingers. Small mercies.

Through the window above the sink, she could see the back garden. Snow lay thick on what might have once been flowerbeds, and a stone wall marked the boundary. Beyond that, fields stretched away towards low hills, everything white and still under a heavy, grey sky.

It was beautiful, in a stark winter kind of way. The kind of beauty that hurt to look at—pure and clean and untouched. She let herself look a moment longer than she meant to, tracing the line of the hills, the pattern of bare branches against white.

Small mercies. There were still small mercies.

Finally, she turned away from the window

She opened the door.

Warmth hit her immediately. Not the blazing heat of the sitting room fire, but a gentler warmth, like stepping into a greenhouse on a spring day. Joanna stood in the doorway, confused, and looked around.

The conservatory was exactly as she'd seen it yesterday—terracotta tiles, glass walls and roof, the single wingback chair angled towards the windows. But it was warm. Properly warm. There were no radiators, no heaters, nothing to explain it.

She stepped inside, and the door swung shut behind her. The warmth wrapped around her like a blanket. Outside the glass, snow was falling in lazy spirals, but in here it felt like a different season entirely.

'This isn't normal,' Joanna said aloud. 'What is it? Perhaps there is underfloor heating?' Her voice sounded small in the quiet space.

The conservatory didn't answer, of course. But the warmth persisted, and after a moment, Joanna walked to the chair and sat down.

It was like coming home to something she had never known.

The chair fitted her perfectly, the curve of the back supporting her spine, the arms at exactly the right height for her elbows. The cushion was soft but not too soft, and when she leaned back and closed her eyes, something in her chest relaxed for the first time in longer than she could remember.

She could have fallen asleep there, and closing her eyes, she fought the urge to give in to sleep. But then she opened her eyes and saw the book.

It was sitting on a small side table she hadn't noticed before—a table that definitely hadn't been there yesterday, she was certain of it. The book was old, its green cloth cover faded and worn smooth by loving hands. No dust jacket. When she picked it up, it fell open to the first page as if it had been read many times, and the paper smelled of vanilla.

A gift. The cottage had given her a gift.

The Secret Garden by Frances Hodgson Burnett.

Joanna hadn't read that story since she was a child. She could barely remember it—something about an orphaned girl and a hidden garden, wasn't it? She turned the page and began to read.

'When Mary Lennox was sent to Misselthwaite Manor to live with her uncle, everybody said she was the most disagreeable-looking child ever seen...'

The words pulled her in. She read one page, then another, then looked up and realised an hour had passed and the light had changed. Snow had stopped falling. A weak sun was trying to break through the clouds.

She'd left her tea in the kitchen; it would be stone cold by now. Joanna stood, marked her place, and went to make fresh tea. When she came back, she settled into the chair again and kept reading.

The cottage was quiet around her. Just the faint crackle of the fire from the sitting room and the occasional creak of old timbers. Safe sounds. Homely sounds.

By the time the light began to fail, Joanna had read five chapters, and Mary Lennox had discovered the hidden garden's door. Joanna closed the book and sat for a moment, holding it in her lap. Something about the story had caught her—the lonely child, the cold house, the sense that everything was dead and finished until it wasn't.

She put the book back on the side table and stood. Her body ached from sitting so long, but it was a good ache. A comfortable ache.

In the kitchen, she opened another tin— tomato soup this time—and ate it cold because she still couldn't face working out the Aga. She made more tea. Looked out at the darkening garden. The village beyond the garden wall was lighting up, windows glowing gold, smoke rising from chimneys.

She should have a bath. Unpack properly. Work out where the airing cupboard was and find blankets. She should do lots of things.

Instead, Joanna went to the sitting room window and looked out at the green.

The couple from yesterday were there again.

They were walking the same route, arms linked, talking. As Joanna watched, they stopped outside a cottage three doors down from the pub. The woman knocked, and after a moment, the door opened. An older woman appeared, white-haired and beaming, and ushered them inside.

The door closed. The green was empty again.

Joanna pressed her hand against the cold glass. They'd been expected, those two. Welcomed. They belonged here in a way she never would.

The thought should have hurt, but she was too numb for hurt. Just tired. So tired.

She went upstairs, lay down on the bed still fully clothed, and closed her eyes.

The fire kept burning. The cottage kept watch. And Joanna slept.

##

The next day was the same, more or less. Joanna woke cold, went downstairs to the fire that still burned, made tea and ate the rest of the beans in the tin. She told herself she'd go out later. Walk to the village shop, buy fresh food. Real food.

But the conservatory called to her.

She went back to the chair, picked up *The Secret Garden*, and kept reading. Lost herself in Mary Lennox's story—the moor, the robin, the hidden garden coming slowly back to life. It was a children's book, really. Simple. Sentimental. But something about it reached parts of her that had been frozen for a long time.

When she looked up, it was afternoon, and she'd read the same page three times without taking in a word.

Her mind had wandered. Back to Marcus, to the way he'd looked at her that morning as if she was a problem he'd finally worked out how to solve. Back to Mum in the hospital bed, her breathing shallow and rattling. Back further, to Dad calling her name in the night, confused and frightened, and her stumbling downstairs at three a.m. to help him to the bathroom.

Years of it. Years of being needed and useful and essential, and what did it leave her with? This. A freezing cottage, very little money, and a borrowed book she couldn't even focus on.

Joanna closed the book and stood. She should eat. Should do something other than sit here feeling sorry for herself.

She made tea—always tea, as if it could solve anything. Well, tea didn't solve things exactly—but it made them bearable. She stood at the kitchen window, looking out. The sun had broken through properly now, pale and watery but determined. It caught the snow in the garden, and she drew in a breath as it sparkled.

Pretty. That's what people would say. How pretty. How lucky you are.

She turned away from the window.

That's when she saw the herbs.

They were sitting on the windowsill above the sink—three small terracotta pots, each with a different plant growing green and healthy. Rosemary, thyme, and something else she didn't recognise. The scent of them reached her even from across the kitchen, sharp and fresh and alive.

They hadn't been there before, and she certainly hadn't put them there.

Joanna walked slowly to the windowsill and touched one of the plants—the rosemary, its needle-like leaves stiff under her fingers. It was real. Growing. Thriving, even though it was January and everything outside was dead or dormant.

'What are you?' she whispered. Then, touching the soft rosemary leaves again: 'Thank you.'

The cottage didn't answer. But the fire in the sitting room popped warmly, and the conservatory's warmth seemed to reach further into the kitchen, wrapping around her shoulders like a shawl. And Joanna understood, in a way that bypassed logic entirely, that the cottage was trying to help.

More than that, it cared.

The thought should have been frightening. Instead, for the first time in months, she felt the tiniest flicker of something that might have been hope.

Which should have been mad. Was mad. Cottages didn't help people. Fires didn't light themselves. Herbs didn't appear on windowsills.

But they had, and she was too tired to fight it anymore.

The days blurred together. Four of them? Five? Joanna lost count. She woke, made tea, ate beans or soup from a tin, and retreated to the conservatory. To the chair that fitted her so perfectly and the book she couldn't seem to finish. She'd read the same three pages over and over, her mind refusing to hold onto the words, sliding away into memories she didn't want to examine.

She was stuck. The word came to her one afternoon as she sat with the book closed in her lap, staring out at the snow-covered garden. Stuck. Like a scratched record playing the same music over and over.

She needed to move forward. Knew she needed to. But how could she? How did you move forward when you'd spent ten years in reverse, your life shrinking down to hospitals and care homes and the relentless grind of other people's needs?

Through the conservatory's glass walls, she watched as a robin perched on the garden wall. It cocked its head, bright-eyed, then flew away.

She should go out, perhaps at least walk to the village. She'd been living on tinned food for—how long? Nearly a week? That wasn't healthy or normal

But normal seemed like something that belonged to other people now.

Joanna closed her eyes and let the conservatory's warmth soak into her bones. The chair held her gently. The cottage kept watch. And outside, the world went on without her, just as it always had.

##

The next day, Joanna forced herself to get dressed properly. She found clean clothes in her suitcase, had a bath in water that ran surprisingly hot because she still hadn't worked out where the immersion heater was. The cottage, she was starting to realise, ran on its own rules.

She put on jeans and a jumper, brushed her hair until it looked almost presentable, and went downstairs with the intention of walking to the shop.

But the sitting room window caught her attention as she passed.

But the sitting room window caught her attention as she passed.

The couple were there again. The tall man with the dark hair showing silver, and the woman in the purple coat. They were walking slowly around the green, arms linked, talking, their breath misting in the cold air.

As Joanna watched, they stopped outside the cottage three doors down from the pub. The same cottage as before. The older woman—the white-haired one—came out to meet them. She kissed them both on the cheek, gestured for them to come in. The woman in the purple coat said something that made all three of them laugh.

They disappeared inside. The door closed.

And Joanna stood at her window, watching the empty green, and felt the loneliness like a physical weight in her chest.

That's what she wanted. That easy affection, that belonging, that sense of being expected and welcomed and *known*. She'd had it once, or thought she had. Friends from school, friends from work, a husband who'd promised her forever.

But forever had lasted thirteen years, and her friends had drifted away during the years she'd spent caring for her parents, and now there was no one. No one at all.

She turned away from the window and went back to the conservatory.

The book was waiting on the side table. *The Secret Garden*. She picked it up, opened it to where she'd left off—page seventy-three, the same page she'd been staring at for three days—and tried to read.

'It was the sweetest, most mysterious-looking place anyone could imagine...'

The words blurred. She blinked hard, tried again.

'It was the sweetest, most mysterious-looking place...'

She couldn't do this. Couldn't just sit here day after day, reading the same words, eating cold food from tins, hiding from the world. She needed to get out. Needed to do something. Anything.

She needed a different book.

The thought came clearly, cutting through the fog that had been wrapping around her thoughts for days. She needed a different book because she couldn't finish this one, and she couldn't just sit here staring at the same page forever.

There'd been a bookshop. She'd seen it when she'd driven through the village that first day. A bow-windowed shop front with books stacked in the display. It couldn't be far. Nothing in a village this size was far.

Tomorrow. She'd go tomorrow.

Joanna closed the book and set it carefully on the side table. Outside, the light was fading towards evening. Snow had started falling again, soft and thick. She could see lights in the cottages around the green, could imagine the warmth inside them. Families. Friends. Lives that made sense.

She went to make tea—because that's what she did, over and over, as if the ritual could hold her together—and found herself pausing in the kitchen, looking at the herbs on the windowsill. The rosemary, the thyme, the third plant she still didn't recognise. All green and thriving in the middle of winter.

'Thank you,' she said quietly.

The cottage didn't answer, but the conservatory's warmth seemed to pulse just a little stronger, and upstairs, she heard a floorboard creak as if the old building was settling in for the night.

Tomorrow. She'd go to the bookshop tomorrow.

She had to. She couldn't read the same page for the rest of her life.

Could she?

Chapter Three

The church bells woke Joanna the next morning.

She lay in bed, listening to them ring across the village. Deep, resonant tones that seemed to come from everywhere and nowhere, rolling through the cold morning air. They rang with a rhythm she remembered from childhood—call to worship, call to community, call to the faithful to gather.

She had loved going to church when she was a child. The soaring ceilings that made her feel wonderfully small, the coloured light through stained glass, the way the vicar's voice echoed. It had felt like stepping into a magical world every Sunday morning.

Sunday. It must be Sunday.

She'd lost track of the days. Had it been a week since she'd arrived? More? Time had a strange quality here, stretching and contracting as though it had a life of its own. Hours in the conservatory felt like minutes. Days had passed and she couldn't say what she'd done with them.

The bells kept ringing. Joanna pulled the blanket over her head, but couldn't block out the sound. It reached into the small, cold room and demanded attention—there is a world out there.

Finally, she gave up on sleep and got out of bed.

The bedroom window looked out over the front garden and the green beyond. Joanna pulled back the thin curtain and caught her breath.

Snow had fallen thick overnight, transforming everything. The garden was buried under it, the path to the gate invisible, only the dark shapes of what might be rose bushes marking where the flowerbeds had been. The gate had a cap of snow, softening the iron scrollwork. Beyond, the green was a pristine expanse of white, unmarked except for a single set of fox prints cutting diagonally across towards the pub.

The village looked like something from a Victorian painting. Every rooftop carried its burden of snow, every windowsill, every garden wall. Smoke rose from chimneys in straight grey lines—no wind this morning, just still, cold air and the gentle fall of fresh flakes. They drifted down lazy and fat, the kind of snow that made no sound, just accumulated in silence.

And there, beyond the cluster of cottages, rising above the bare trees at the far edge of the village, was the church spire.

It was perfect. Absolutely perfect. Like a painting she could step into and leave all her grief behind.

Joanna hadn't noticed it before, or perhaps, hadn't let herself notice it. But this morning, with snow falling and the bells ringing, she couldn't look away. The spire was grey stone, pointing up towards low clouds like a finger raised in prayer. A weathervane topped it— though it was hard to see what it was clearly through the snow.

The bells rang from that tower. She could almost see the sound and could feel it vibrating through the cold air, through the glass, through her chest where memories stirred reluctantly to life.

It was perfect. Absolutely perfect. Like a painting she could step into and leave all her grief behind.

Joanna pressed her hand to the glass and smiled despite herself. However lost she felt, however broken, the world could still be beautiful. That had to mean something.

She'd married Marcus in a church. Not in her home village of Hay-on-Wye—his mother had insisted on the parish church near their family home in Surrey. Joanna had worn white silk and carried roses and walked down an aisle between pews packed with his relatives while her own small family sat near the back, self-conscious and out of place. The bells had rung then, too, joyfully announcing to the world that Joanna Davies was now Joanna Hartwell and her life was about to begin properly.

Twenty-three years ago. She'd been twenty-eight. Young enough to believe that love was enough, that saying forever did mean forever.

But the bells here sounded different. Older, maybe. Less certain. Or perhaps that was just her, hearing them through the filter of her life.

As she watched, people began to emerge from cottages around the green. An elderly couple, moving carefully on the snowy path. A family with two children bundled in bright coats. A woman with white hair who walked with a stick but moved purposefully towards the church. They called greetings to each other, their voices carrying in the cold air. A man stopped to help the elderly couple navigate a slippery patch.

Community. That's what this was. The word felt like something from another language.

Joanna turned away from the window. She couldn't bear to watch anymore.

Downstairs, the fire was burning as it always did now, as if the cottage had given up pretending to be normal. Logs appeared without her touching the basket—she never saw it happen, but the fire was always fed, always burning, the woodpile beside the hearth never diminishing, no matter how many days passed. She went to the kitchen and made tea, and while the kettle boiled, she stood at the back window and looked out at the garden. It was bigger than she'd thought earlier. The snow revealed its shape—a rectangle perhaps thirty feet deep, bounded by the stone wall on three sides and the cottage on the fourth. What she'd taken for shapeless mounds were actually structured beds, their edges just visible under the snow. Near the back wall stood an apple tree, its bare branches black against the white. Over the stone wall at the back, she could see an apple orchard.

Someone had loved this garden once. Had planted those beds, chosen that tree, placed that birdbath just so. Someone had sat in the conservatory on summer mornings and watched things grow. Had it been Victoria, her cousin or someone else who had lived here before her cousin?

The kettle clicked off. Joanna made her tea and carried it through to the conservatory.

The warmth enveloped her immediately. She sank into the chair—her chair now, that's how she thought of it—and looked out at the transformed garden. From here, the view was different. She could see past the back wall to the fields beyond, white and undulating towards distant hills. The sky was pale grey, heavy with more snow, but here and there, breaks in the cloud revealed glimpses of silver light.

The Secret Garden sat on the side table where she'd left it. Joanna picked it up, opened it to page seventy-three, and tried to read.

'It was the sweetest, most mysterious-looking place anyone could imagine...'

No. Still no. The words were there, but they

wouldn't connect to anything in her mind. She closed the book with a snap that sounded too loud in the quiet space.

She needed to go to the bookshop. She'd said she'd go yesterday and hadn't managed it. Today. She'd go today, church bells or no church bells.

Joanna set down her mug and was about to stand when something moved in the garden.

The robin landed on the birdbath, sending up a small puff of snow, and looked directly at her through the glass. Its bright red breast stood out against all that white. They regarded each other for a long moment, woman and bird, and then it flew to the apple tree, perched on a low branch, and began to sing.

The sound pierced through the glass, clear and sweet and heartbreakingly beautiful. The robin sang with its whole small body, throat vibrating, tail twitching, claiming territory or calling for a mate or simply celebrating the morning.

Joanna found herself smiling. Really smiling, for the first time since she could remember. 'Hello, little friend,' she whispered.

The robin sang louder, as if answering.

Her tears came without warning, hot and sudden. She pressed her hands to her face but couldn't stop them. They spilled through her fingers and down her wrists, soaking into her jumper sleeves. She cried silently, shoulders shaking, while the robin sang and the snow fell and the church bells rang their Sunday call in the distance.

She cried for the garden someone had loved. For the cottage that was trying so hard to help her. For the village full of strangers who had each other, while she had no one. For the life she'd thought she'd have and the one she'd ended up with instead. For her parents, dead within months of each other, and Marcus, who'd stopped loving her long before he'd left, and the years she'd spent being useful instead of being herself because she'd forgotten there was a difference.

The robin finished its song and flew away. The bells stopped ringing. And Joanna sat in the warm conservatory and cried until there was nothing left.

##

The knock came at eleven o'clock.

Joanna had washed her face with cold water,

made more tea and told herself firmly to stop being ridiculous. It was time to get some proper food in. Real food, not beans from a tin. She needed to go to the shop, and maybe find the bookshop if she was brave enough. She needed to do something other than sit in this cottage and fall apart.

The knock came just as she was pulling on her coat.

She froze in the hallway. No one knew she was here. Well, the solicitor knew, but no one else. No one who would knock on her door on a Sunday morning.

The knock came again. Firm but not impatient. The sound of someone who would wait.

Joanna opened the door.

The woman on the doorstep was perhaps seventy, with white hair pinned in a soft bun and a face that suggested she smiled often. She wore a thick wool coat in forest green and held a wicker basket covered with a tea towel. Her eyes were sharp, yet kind in equal measure, and they took Joanna in with a single sweeping glance that saw everything—the unwashed hair, the too-thin frame, the eyes puffy from crying.

'My dear,' the woman said warmly. 'I'm Mrs Willoughby from Rose Cottage, three doors down. I do hope you don't mind the intrusion, but I wanted to welcome you to the village. I gave you a little time to settle in.'

Joanna's throat closed. She managed something that might have been a smile, might have been a grimace. 'That's... thank you. I'm Joanna.'

'What a lovely name.' Mrs Willoughby's smile didn't waver. 'I've brought a few things. Just some soup and fresh bread, and a jar of my honey. Nothing grand, but I thought you might appreciate it.'

She held out the basket, and Joanna took it automatically, the weight of it pulling at her arms. It was heavier than she'd expected. Real food. Proper food. Her eyes pricked with fresh tears, and she blinked hard.

'Thank you,' she managed. 'That's very kind of you.'

'Not at all.' Mrs Willoughby tilted her head slightly, studying her. 'I hope you're settling in? Hawthorn Cottage can be a bit particular, but it has a good heart.'

Something in the way she said it made

Joanna look up sharply. Mrs Willoughby's expression was mild, pleasant, but her eyes held something else. Knowledge, maybe. Understanding.

'It's...' Joanna started, then stopped. How did you explain that the cottage lit its own fires? That it filled itself with warmth when she was cold? That herbs appeared on windowsills and chairs positioned themselves, and it all should have been terrifying, but somehow wasn't?

'It's been empty too long,' Mrs Willoughby said gently. 'The cottage, I mean. It's glad you're here.'

The words hung between them. *Glad*. As if cottages could be glad.

'I think...' Joanna's voice came out hoarse. 'I think things are happening. Things that shouldn't. The fire just... and it's warm when it shouldn't be, and I thought I was...'

She couldn't finish. Couldn't say the words, *going mad* to this kind stranger on her doorstep.

Mrs Willoughby stepped closer and put a warm hand on Joanna's arm. 'My dear, may I come in? Just for a moment. I think we should talk.'

Joanna nodded, not trusting her voice, and

stepped back to let her in.

Mrs Willoughby crossed the threshold and looked around the hallway with the air of someone greeting an old friend. 'Yes,' she murmured. 'Yes, there you are. I thought as much.'

She turned to Joanna, who stood clutching the basket like a shield. 'You're not going mad, dear. I promise you that. The cottage is... well, it's special. Has been for longer than anyone can remember. It takes care of people who need taking care of.'

'But that's not...' Joanna shook her head. 'That's not possible.'

'Isn't it?' Mrs Willoughby moved past her into the sitting room, where the fire burned cheerfully in the grate. She held out her hands to warm them, completely unsurprised. 'Our village has always had a bit of magic to it. Quiet magic, nothing showy. Just things that help when help is needed. The cottage is one of those things.'

Magic. The word should have sounded absurd. Should have made her question Mrs Willoughby's sanity instead of her own. But standing here in the hallway with a basket of food in her arms and the fire crackling and the conservatory's warmth reaching around her like an embrace, Joanna found she believed it.

'I don't understand,' she whispered.

'You don't need to understand.' Mrs Willoughby turned to her with a smile. 'You just need to accept. Let the cottage help you. That's what it wants to do.'

'Why?' The question burst out of her. 'Why would it want to help me?'

'Because you need help, dear. And because that's what it does.' Mrs Willoughby gestured around the room. 'This cottage has housed dozens of souls over the past two centuries. People who were lost, or hurt, or starting over. It gives them what they need—warmth, safety, time. And when they're ready, when they're healed enough, they move on. The cottage lets them go and waits for the next one.'

She paused, tilted her head. 'Though I wonder if perhaps this time is different. Victoria leaving it to you specifically—that wasn't random, dear. The cottage has been waiting. And now you own it. That means something.'

Joanna set the basket down carefully on the hall table before her shaking hands could drop it. 'I can't keep it. I'll sell it as soon as I work out where to go next. Use the money to start over somewhere else.'

'Of course.' Mrs Willoughby's tone was placid, as if it didn't matter one way or another. 'But while you're here, let it help. Don't fight it. That only makes things harder. And don't make any hasty decisions about selling. The cottage will let you know when the time is right. If the time is right. Come to tea on Thursday. Nothing formal—I've invited Vivian and Dimity from Pippins Nook as well. They've been wanting to meet you. Vivian makes excellent cake when he's in the mood; he might bring one of his famous Victoria sponges.' She smiled warmly. 'They've been wanting to meet you properly. We all have.'

Joanna's throat tightened. 'I don't know—'

'Three o'clock,' Mrs Willoughby said firmly. 'Rose Cottage, the one with the red door. You can't miss it. And do come, dear. We don't bite. Well, Dimity might ask a lot of questions, but that's just her way.'

She paused at the door, then turned back with a knowing smile. 'I hear you've been reading. The cottage tells me these things—

what books appear, what someone needs. It's rather good at knowing.'

Joanna blinked. 'How do you—'

'Dimity's an author, you know. Quite famous. You should look for her books when you visit the bookshop; Hugh has them all. Romantasy. Isn't that a wonderful word?' Mrs Willoughby's eyes twinkled.

She was gone before Joanna could respond, leaving behind the basket and the scent of honey and bread, and a strange lightness in the cottage's atmosphere, as if it was pleased with how things had gone.

Joanna stood in the hallway for a long moment, staring at the closed door. Magic. The cottage was magic. The village had magic. And she wasn't going mad.

The relief hit her so hard her knees went weak. She sat down abruptly on the stairs and put her head in her hands. Not mad. Just staying in an enchanted cottage in a village that defied every law of nature she'd ever learned.

She started to laugh. Couldn't help it. The sound came out high and slightly hysterical, echoing in the hallway, but it felt good. Better than crying. Better than the numb silence she'd been wrapped in for days.

The fire popped in the sitting room. The conservatory's warmth reached towards her. And Joanna sat on the stairs in Hawthorn Cottage and laughed until her sides hurt, while outside the snow kept falling and the church spire pointed skyward and the village went about its magical Sunday. She didn't get to the village that day.

Chapter Four

Joanna ate Mrs Willoughby's soup for lunch on Monday, and again for dinner. It was chicken and vegetable, thick with pearl barley, the kind of soup that tasted like someone had put care into making it. She heated it on the electric hob—still couldn't face working out the Aga—and ate it standing at the kitchen counter, looking out at the snow-covered garden. Her energy returned, and her mind was sharp and clear.

The robin came back. It perched on the apple tree and sang to her. This time, Joanna didn't cry. She just watched and listened, and smiled.

Beyond the back wall, she could see the hill rising behind the village. She hadn't noticed it properly before. But this morning, with clearer skies, it dominated the view—a gentle slope covered in snow, with bare trees scattered across its flank and a copse of dark pines near the summit. It protected the village, cradled between the hill at its back and the fields stretching away to the front.

Tuesday, she finished the soup and started on the bread, which was dense and grainy and so much better than anything from a tin that she ate three slices slathered with butter and Mrs Willoughby's honey. The honey was dark and rich, tasting of summer and flowers she couldn't name.

She didn't go to the bookshop that day either. Told herself she would, but when it came to putting on her coat and opening the door, she couldn't make herself do it.

Wednesday was the same. She sat in the conservatory with *The Secret Garden* open in her lap, staring at page seventy-three, and the cottage sighed around her in a way that felt almost disappointed in her.

'I know,' she told it. 'I know.'

But knowing didn't help.

Thursday morning, she woke to pale sunshine breaking through the clouds. The first real sun since she'd arrived. It slanted through the bedroom window and fell across the bed in a bright rectangle, warm enough that she could feel it through the blankets.

Downstairs, the conservatory was flooded

with light. The chair positioned in its path caught the sun perfectly, and when Joanna sat down—because she always sat down, because the chair called to her and she couldn't refuse—the warmth soaked through her jumper and into her skin.

She picked up *The Secret Garden* again. Opened it to page seventy-three. Read the same words she'd been staring at for over a week.

'It was the sweetest, most mysterious-looking place anyone could imagine...'

And this time, finally, something in her broke open.

She couldn't do this anymore. Couldn't sit here day after day, frozen in place, reading the same page like a broken record. The cottage was trying to help her—Mrs Willoughby had said as much, and Joanna believed it now—but she had to meet it halfway. Had to try.

She closed the book with a decisive snap and stood up.

The bookshop. She was going to the bookshop.

Right now, before she could talk herself out of it again.

##

The village was transformed by sunshine. Everything that had looked grey and forbidding under snow-laden clouds now sparkled and gleamed brightly. The snow on the green was pristine except for a maze of footprints where children had played, and icicles hung from eaves like delicate crystal decorations. The church spire caught the light glowing against the pale blue sky.

Joanna walked slowly, careful on the icy path. She'd put on her good coat, navy wool that had seen better days—and a scarf she'd found in the cottage, which had probably belonged to Victoria. Her boots weren't really adequate for snow, but they'd have to do.

As she reached the front gate, she heard the gentle sound of water running. She paused, listening, then looked to her right.

A millstream ran along the far side of the lane, separating the row of cottages from the rising ground beyond. She'd been too wrapped up in herself to notice it before, but now she could hear it clearly, that persistent musical sound of water flowing over stone. The stream was perhaps six feet across, its banks edged with snow, but the water itself ran dark and quick, too fast to freeze. A small stone bridge crossed it further down, near where the lane curved towards the church.

The sound was soothing. Constant. It made the village feel older somehow, as if it had been here forever, water flowing and seasons turning while happiness and sadness came and went.

Joanna stood listening for a moment, then turned left onto the lane and started walking.

The cold air hurt her lungs. She wasn't used to it. Wasn't used to being outside at all, she realised. How long had it been? Ten days? Nearly two weeks? She'd barely been outside the cottage since she'd arrived.

People were out. A woman was sweeping snow from her front path. Two men stood talking outside the pub, their breath misting. An elderly lady walked past with a shopping bag, smiled at Joanna, and said, 'Lovely morning.'

Joanna managed a nod in return, kept walking.

The millstream accompanied her, running parallel to the lane. She could see how it had shaped the village—cottages built on its near bank, the land on the far side rising towards the hill. The hill itself loomed larger now that she was near it, its slope gentle but definite, crowned with those dark pines that stood out stark against the snow. Sheep tracks zigzagged across its white face, and she could just make out a few hardy ewes grazing near the tree line, dark shapes against all that white.

The bookshop was on the far side of the green, tucked between a tea room and what looked like a general store. She'd noticed it that first day, driving through, but up close it was even more charming. The leaded bow windows were old, the glass wavy with age, and they were stacked with books arranged artfully around a display of local interest titles. A hand-painted sign above the door read *Chapter & Verse* in elegant script.

Joanna stood on the pavement, staring at it. Her heart was hammering as if she was about to do something dangerous instead of just entering a shop.

But it felt dangerous. Felt like stepping back into the world after hiding from it. Felt like admitting she needed something—needed books, needed stories, needed something beyond the walls of Hawthorn Cottage.

The doorbell chimed when she pushed the

door open. The sound was bright and welcoming, and it announced her to the man behind the counter, who looked up and smiled.

'Good morning,' he said. 'Please, have a browse. Let me know if you need any assistance.'

His voice was quiet, not pushing. Joanna nodded and moved quickly past him, deeper into the shop, before he could see how her face had flushed.

The bookshop was small but beautifully organised. Shelves lined every wall, floor to ceiling, and more shelves marched down the centre in neat rows. A wood-burning stove crackled in one corner, and an old leather armchair was positioned beside it. The air smelled of paper and woodsmoke and coffee, and somewhere classical music played quietly—piano, something gentle she didn't recognise.

Joanna wandered between the shelves, not really seeing the titles. Her hands were shaking. This was ridiculous. She was fifty-one years old, not a frightened child. She could buy a book. It was a simple transaction. She'd done it a thousand times before.

But that was before. Before Marcus, before caregiving, before she'd become this person who couldn't even finish a children's novel without falling apart.

She stopped in front of the fiction section and made herself focus. Read the spines. Contemporary, classics, crime, historical. Too many choices. She couldn't think.

'Can I help you find something?'

Joanna spun around. The man from the counter had come up behind her—not close, keeping a respectful distance, but she hadn't heard him approach. He was perhaps a similar age to her, tall but slightly stooped, as if he spent a lot of time bending over books. Grey hair, slightly tousled as though he'd run his hands through it while reading. Kind eyes behind wire-rimmed glasses. He wore a navy cardigan over a pale blue shirt and red tie, very proper, very bookish.

'I...' Her voice came out as barely a whisper. She cleared her throat, tried again. 'I need something new. To read.'

His smile was gentle. 'Well, you've come to the right place. What sort of thing do you enjoy?'

'I don't... I'm not sure.' She could feel heat creeping up her neck. 'I've been trying to read *The Secret Garden,* but I can't... I keep getting stuck.'

She didn't know why she'd told him that. It sounded pathetic.

But he just nodded thoughtfully. 'Lovely book, but sometimes we need something different. What is it about *The Secret Garden* that's not working for you?'

Joanna looked at her hands. 'I can't concentrate. I read the same page over and over, and nothing goes in.'

'Ah.' He was quiet for a moment, considering. 'That happens sometimes. Usually means we need something that pulls us in harder, something we can't look away from.' He moved along the shelf, running his finger along the spines. 'Or sometimes we need something lighter. Something that gives instead of takes.'

He pulled out a book and handed it to her. *The Enchanted April* by Elizabeth von Arnim.

'Try this,' he said. 'It's about four women who rent a castle in Italy for a month. They're all stuck in different ways, all a bit lost. But the place—and each other—help them find themselves again.'

Joanna took the book. The cover was pretty, watercolour washes of pink and gold. She turned it over, read the back, and felt something stir in her chest.

'It's about giving yourself permission to bloom again,' the man said quietly. 'After a long winter.'

Their eyes met. His were grey-blue, serious but warm, and in them she saw something she recognised—loss, grief, and difficult times. He understood. Somehow, this stranger in a bookshop understood.

'Thank you,' she managed.

'Hugh Morrison,' he said, holding out his hand. 'I'm the owner here. I moved back to the village a few years ago.'

Joanna shook his hand. His grip was warm, careful. 'Joanna Hartwell. I'm... I'm staying at Hawthorn Cottage.'

'Ah, Victoria Davies' place. I'm sorry for your loss—she was a lovely woman.'

'Thank you. Though I barely knew her, honestly. We only met once.'

'Still. She clearly thought of you. Leaving

you the cottage.'

The way he said it, so casually, as if magical cottages were perfectly normal, made her laugh. The sound surprised them both.

'I'm starting to realise that,' she said.

His smile widened. 'This village has always been a bit special. You'll get used to it.' He stepped back, giving her space. 'Will that be all today, or can I find you anything else?'

'Just this.' She held up *The Enchanted April*. 'How much do I owe you?'

'Seven fifty.'

She paid—notes from her dwindling supply of cash—and he wrapped the book in brown paper with string, his movements deft—he had beautiful hands. When he handed the package to her, their fingers brushed. Just for a second, just a brief touch of skin on skin, but it sent something like electricity running up her arm.

Joanna pulled back, clutching the wrapped book to her chest. 'Thank you. For the recommendation.'

'You're very welcome.' Was it her imagination, or did his voice sound slightly different? Rougher? 'I hope you enjoy it. And if you don't, come back and I'll find you something else. That's my guarantee.'

She nodded, couldn't speak, and fled towards the door. The bell chimed again as she pushed through, and then she was outside in the cold, bright air, breathing hard, her face hot despite the temperature.

What was wrong with her? He'd been kind, helpful, nothing more. There was no reason for her heart to be racing, for her skin to feel too tight, for that brief touch to still be humming through her nerves.

She started walking back towards Hawthorn Cottage, head down, the wrapped book pressed against her chest like a charm.

The millstream burbled alongside the lane. She crossed the small stone bridge without really seeing it, her mind too full of grey-blue eyes and careful hands and a voice that had said *after a long winter* as if he knew exactly how long her winter had been.

##

Hugh watched her go.

She was halfway across the green before he moved, and then he turned back to the counter and stood there, gripping its edge, staring at nothing.

What had just happened?

She'd been in his shop for perhaps ten minutes. She hadn't said more than a few sentences. She'd been nervous, clearly, possibly scared—of what, he couldn't begin to guess—and there'd been something fragile about her that made him want to help, to ease whatever burden she was carrying.

But that wasn't all he'd felt.

When their fingers had touched, when she'd looked up at him with those dark eyes that held too much pain, he'd felt something he hadn't felt since Sarah was alive. Something that pulled at him, made him notice details he had no business noticing. The way her dark hair—brown shot through with silver—fell across her face in a soft wave she kept tucking behind her ear. The delicate curve of her jaw. The shape of her mouth, full-lipped and expressive even when she wasn't speaking. Her skin was pale, almost translucent in the winter light, the kind of complexion that showed every emotion, every sleepless night. Fine lines bracketed her eyes and mouth—laughter lines, he thought, though they looked as if they hadn't been used for a long time. And her voice, when she'd said she kept getting stuck, had held such quiet desperation that he'd wanted to promise her she wouldn't stay stuck. That he'd help her move forward. He'd wanted to help her. God, he'd wanted to help her.

And he had no right to want anything of the sort.

Sarah had been gone for four years. Four years of him and Emma rebuilding their lives, learning how to be just the two of them, finding some kind of peace in the wreckage. Four years, and he hadn't looked at another woman. Hadn't wanted to. Had told himself that chapter of his life was closed.

But Joanna Hartwell had walked into his shop, and something in him had woken up unbidden.

He thought of Sarah at the end. The hospital bed in their sitting room because she'd wanted to be home. The way she'd looked at him one morning—lucid, for the first time in days—and told him it was all right. That when she was gone, he should live. Should be happy. She had made him promise that he would.

And he did. Had held her hand and lied through his tears and promised.

But sitting in that room day after day, watching her slip away, he'd sometimes thought: please, let it be over. Please, let this end. For her sake and—God forgive him—for his.

He'd hated himself for those thoughts. Still hated himself.

And now a woman with sad eyes had touched his hand, and he'd felt alive for the first time in years, and the guilt was crushing.

'Dad?'

Hugh looked up. Emma was standing in the doorway that led to the back room and their flat above, school bag over her shoulder. She'd been upstairs doing homework.

'You okay?' she asked. 'You look weird.'

He managed a smile. 'I'm fine, love. Just wool-gathering.'

'Who was that lady?'

A customer. New to the village, I think. Staying at Hawthorn Cottage.'

Emma's eyes went wide. 'Really? In another one of the magic cottages?'

'Don't call them that,' Hugh said automatically, though everyone in the village knew certain cottages were different. Hawthorn

Cottage, Pippin's Nook next door, Rose Cottage down the lane—those and others all had their peculiarities. 'They're just old.'

'They're magic,' Emma insisted. She came closer, lowered her voice conspiratorially. 'Gran says people who stay in those cottages are always a bit broken. And the cottages fix them. Like how Dimity got her sight back at Pippin's Nook, and Mrs Willoughby found peace at Rose Cottage after her awful marriage.'

'Emma—'

'I liked her,' Emma said. 'She looked sad. I hope Hawthorn Cottage helps her. It's been waiting for someone, Gran said. Been empty too long.'

Hugh looked out the bow window. Joanna was gone now, vanished back into Hawthorn Cottage, probably. He wondered if she'd read the book. If it would help.

If he'd see her again.

'Dad?' Emma was watching him with that too-perceptive look she'd developed since Sarah died. 'Are you sure you're okay?'

'I'm sure.' He ruffled her hair, made his voice light. 'Come on, let's close up early, and I'll make us tea. What do you fancy—fish fingers?'

'Pizza?'

Hugh shook his head. Emma wrinkled her nose but followed him towards the back room, already chattering about something that had happened at school. He listened with half his attention, the rest of it still on a woman with dark hair and frightened eyes who kept getting stuck on the same page.

He hoped she wouldn't get stuck anymore.

He hoped he'd see her again.

And then he felt guilty for hoping.

##

Joanna closed the cottage door behind her and leaned against it, breathing hard. The fire was burning cheerfully in the sitting room. The conservatory's warmth reached towards her. The cottage welcomed her home.

'Hello,' she said quietly.

She unwrapped the book with shaking hands. *The Enchanted April*. Her fingers still tingled where Hugh Morrison's fingers had brushed hers. She could still see his kind eyes and hear his quiet voice talking about giving yourself permission to bloom.

She carried the book through to the

conservatory and stopped dead.

On the windowsill, in a simple terracotta pot that definitely hadn't been there this morning, sat a single amaryllis bulb. It had already started to grow. A thick green shoot pushed up from the soil, vital and alive, and at its tip she could see the promise of a bud forming.

No way. Amaryllis took weeks to bloom. This one was growing as she watched, or felt like it was. The shoot was perhaps four inches tall already, sturdy and strong, reaching towards the light.

Beyond the conservatory glass, she could see the garden wall and the fields beyond, and rising above them all, the hill with its crown of dark pines. The millstream was just audible, a constant gentle sound that spoke of continuity, of water that had run here for centuries and would run for centuries more. The village nestled in its fold between stream and hill, protected and peaceful, and for the first time since she'd arrived, Joanna felt like she might— just might—belong here. She felt safe, protected.

She touched the amaryllis gently. The leaves were cool and smooth under her fingers, but she could feel the life in them, the determination to grow and bloom and be beautiful even in the depths of winter.

'Thank you,' she whispered to the cottage.

The warmth pulsed, just slightly, like a heartbeat.

She sat in her chair and opened *The Enchanted April* to the first page.

'*It began in a Woman's Club in London on a February afternoon—an uncomfortable club...*'

The words pulled her in immediately. She read one page, then another, then looked up and realised an hour had passed and the light had changed and she'd read thirty pages without stopping once.

Outside, the sun was setting, painting the snow pink and gold. The hill had turned purple in the fading light, the pines black silhouettes against the sky. The amaryllis stood on the windowsill, already taller. And Joanna sat in her warm chair in the magic cottage and read about women who gave themselves permission to recognise who they really were, and for the first time in longer than she could remember, hope trickled through her.

Chapter Five

The book saved Joanna.

She read *The Enchanted April* in two days, curled in the conservatory chair while snow fell outside and the amaryllis grew impossibly taller on the windowsill. She read about women who gave themselves permission to be happy, to bloom. And something in her heart, something that had been frozen for so long she'd forgotten it was there, began very slowly to thaw.

The cottage seemed pleased. The fires burned brighter. Tea tasted better, even though she was still using the same cheap teabags from Tesco. The conservatory's warmth wrapped around her like approval.

On the third morning after her visit to the village, Joanna woke before dawn.

She lay in bed, listening to the absolute silence of deep winter, and felt something pulling at her. Not the conservatory this time. Something else. Something outside.

She got up and went to the window. The sky

was still dark, but there was a quality to the darkness that spoke of approaching light. Stars were fading. The hill behind the village was a black silhouette against deep blue, and as she watched, the faintest hint of gold touched its eastern edge.

Go, something whispered. The cottage, maybe. Or herself. She couldn't tell anymore.

Joanna dressed quickly—jeans, jumper, her inadequate coat, and boots, and then wrapped Victoria's scarf around her neck. She hurried downstairs, where the fire burned welcomingly even though it was barely five in the morning, and let herself out the front door.

The cold hit her like a slap. She gasped, breath fogging white, and nearly turned back. But the eastern sky was lightening, gold bleeding into indigo, and she walked forward.

The lane was empty. Nothing stirred except her boots crunching on yesterday's snow. The millstream was running; that constant musical sound felt like familiar company. Like the village was awake even when it slept, water flowing and earth breathing and everything waiting for the sun.

Joanna turned right at the stone bridge and

followed a footpath that led away from the cottages, across a field towards the hill. Her breath came hard. She wasn't fit; she hadn't walked properly in years. But she kept going, her boots leaving dark tracks across pristine snow as the sky above brightened.

The path climbed. Not steeply, but steadily, and her thighs burned, and her lungs ached, and she had to stop twice to catch her breath. But each time she stopped, she turned to look back at the village, and each time it was more beautiful.

The cottages clustered around the green, smoke rising from chimneys in straight lines. The church spire. The millstream catching the first light like a silver ribbon. And beyond, fields rolling away towards distant horizons, everything white and still and perfect.

She kept climbing.

By the time she reached the copse of pines near the summit, the sun was rising properly. It broke over the far hills in a flood of gold and orange and pink, painting the snow, turning the world into something from a painting. Joanna stood among the dark trees, breathing hard, and watched the sky catch fire.

It was the most beautiful thing she'd seen in many years.

She sank onto a fallen log, not caring that it was covered in snow, and let the tears come. But these weren't the broken tears from before. These were different. These were the tears of someone who'd forgotten the world could be beautiful and was just remembering.

The sun climbed. The sky turned from gold to pale blue. A robin landed on a branch nearby and sang, and Joanna laughed through her tears because of course, there was a robin. There was always a robin now.

'Hello, little robin.'

She sat until her legs were numb from the cold, and she had to stand, stamping feeling back into her feet. The village was properly awake now. She could see people moving about, smoke thickening from chimneys, a car crawling carefully down the lane.

Time to go back.

The walk down was easier, though her legs shook. But she had left something behind at the top of the hill. She was lighter in spirit and had left some of her burden on the hilltop with the sunrise.

##

Mrs Willoughby was waiting on the doorstep when Joanna got back.

She didn't look surprised to see Joanna coming from the hill path, snow-covered and pink-cheeked. She smiled and held up a basket.

'Scones,' she said. 'Still warm. I thought you might like them for breakfast.'

Joanna's throat went tight. 'How did you know I'd be awake?'

'The cottage told me.' Mrs Willoughby said it as if it were perfectly normal. 'Well, not in words, of course. But I've lived here long enough to know when Hawthorn Cottage has something to celebrate. You went up the hill.'

It wasn't a question

'I did.' Joanna fumbled for her key and let them both inside. The cottage was warm, welcoming. The fire crackled hello. 'I don't know why. I just... needed to.'

'The cottage knew you were ready.' Mrs Willoughby followed her through to the kitchen, set the basket on the table. 'First steps are always hardest. You've taken several now.'

Joanna filled the kettle, set it to boil. Her hands were still shaking, but not from the cold.

From something else. Confidence? Hope? 'It was beautiful. The sunrise.'

'It always is, but we forget to look.' Mrs Willoughby sat at the table, made herself at home. 'You'll go again, I expect.'

'Maybe.' Joanna got out mugs and teabags. 'I'm going to return the book today. The one Hugh Morrison recommended.'

'Ah.' Mrs Willoughby's smile widened. 'How lovely. Did you enjoy it?'

'I did. I finished it. I actually finished it.' The relief in her own voice surprised her. 'I haven't been able to finish a book in months. Maybe years.'

'Progress,' Mrs Willoughby said gently. 'The cottage is helping, but you're doing the work. Don't forget that, dear. Magic can open doors, but you have to choose to walk through them.'

They had tea and warm scones with butter and honey, and Mrs Willoughby told her about the village—who lived where, who'd been here for generations, who'd arrived recently. She talked about Vivian and Dimity, how they'd found each other, and how Pippins Nook cottage had helped them. How the village had a way of bringing people together when they needed it most.

'Hugh Morrison? What about him?' Joanna said, trying to sound casual. 'Has he been here long?'

'Came back about four years ago.' Mrs Willoughby's eyes were knowing. 'Grew up in the village, moved away for work, came back after his wife died. Poor man. It was very hard. Emma was only eight. But they're doing better now. He's a good father, and a very kind man.'

Joanna nodded, not trusting herself to say more.

Mrs Willoughby finished her tea and stood. 'I'll leave you to it. But do come for tea tomorrow afternoon. Three o'clock. I meant what I said. We'd all love to meet you properly.'

'I'll try,' Joanna said, and this time she meant it.

##

She waited until the afternoon before going to the bookshop. She spent the morning in the conservatory, watching the amaryllis grow—it was extraordinary. The stalk was nearly a foot tall now, thick and sturdy, and the bud at its tip was swelling visibly. Soon it would open. Blood-red blooms in the depths of winter, growing in defiance of every law of nature.

Just like her, maybe. Growing in defiance of everything that said she was too broken, too old, too damaged.

That thought made her smile.

At two o'clock, she put on her coat, wrapped the book carefully, and walked to the bookshop.

Chapter & Verse looked inviting in the afternoon light. The windows were steamed up from the warmth inside, and through the glass she could see movement. People. More than one person.

Joanna almost turned back. But the book was warm in her hands—or maybe her hands were warm from carrying it—and she thought about the sunrise that morning, and what Mrs Willoughby said about choosing to walk through open doors. She pushed the door open.

The doorbell chimed. Hugh looked up from behind the counter, where he was helping a customer, and his face did something complicated when he saw her. Surprise, pleasure, something else she couldn't quite name.

'Be with you in just a moment,' he said.

Joanna nodded and moved deeper into the shop, pretending to browse. But she was acutely aware of him, of the quiet rumble of his voice as he talked to the other customer, of the way the shop smelled like coffee and old paper and something else, something warm she couldn't identify.

The customer left. The bell chimed again. And then it was just the two of them at the counter.

'Joanna.' Hugh walked out and joined her. He was wearing that same cardigan, his glasses slightly askew. 'You came back.'

'I finished the book.' She held it out. 'You were right. It was exactly what I needed. Thank you.'

He took it, their fingers brushing again, and that same electricity shot up her arm. She pulled back quickly.

'I'm so glad.' He was smiling properly now, and it transformed his face. Made him look younger. 'Did it help? With the getting stuck?'

'Yes.' The word came out fierce, almost defiant. 'I read it in two days. I couldn't put it down. I haven't been able to do that in... I can't remember how long.'

'Sometimes the right book finds us at exactly the right time.' He set it on the counter, gestured to the shelves. 'Would you like another? Or are you taking a break?'

'I'd like another.' Joanna surprised herself with how certain she sounded. 'If you have recommendations.'

'Always.' He moved towards the fiction section, she followed. 'What did you connect with in *The Enchanted April*? That might help me narrow it down.'

Joanna thought about it. 'The... the permission. To want things. To be happy. The idea that places can heal you if you let them.'

Hugh nodded slowly. His eyes were serious behind his glasses. 'Have you found that? With Hawthorn Cottage?'

'I think so. Yes.' She looked at her hands. 'It's strange. The cottage is... helping me. I know how that sounds.'

'It doesn't sound strange at all.' His voice was gentle. 'Not here. Not in this village.'

He led her through the bookshelves and stopped before he pulled a book from the shelf. *The Shell Seekers* by Rosamunde Pilcher. 'Try this. It's about a woman looking back over her life, finding peace with her choices. And it's about art, and family, and second chances.'

Joanna took it. 'Second chances,' she repeated.

'We all deserve them,' Hugh said quietly. 'Even when we think we don't.'

They stood there in the narrow aisle between bookcases, not quite looking at each other, the book warm between them. The silence stretched, not uncomfortable but charged with something.

'Dad?'

A girl appeared from the back room. Twelve or so, all long limbs and dark hair pulled back in a ponytail. She had Hugh's eyes but a sharper chin, a more determined set to her mouth.

'Emma, love.' Hugh stepped back, breaking whatever had been building between them. 'This is Joanna. She's staying at Hawthorn Cottage.'

'The magic cottage,' Emma said immediately, and grinned at Joanna's expression. 'Everyone knows it's magic. It's brilliant. Are you being healed?'

'Emma,' Hugh said, a warning in his voice.

But Joanna laughed. Couldn't help it. The girl's directness was refreshing. 'I think I might be. Maybe.'

'Good.' Emma came closer, studying her with unnerving intensity. 'You look sad. But less sad than you probably did before. That's how it works. The cottage makes you less sad bit by bit until you're not sad anymore.'

'That's quite enough, Em.' Hugh's ears had gone red. 'Joanna doesn't need interrogating.'

'I'm not interrogating. I'm being friendly.' Emma turned to Joanna. 'Do you like books?'

'I do,' Joanna said. 'Very much. Or I used to. I'm remembering how to again.'

'What kind of books?'

'All kinds. But I like stories about people finding themselves. Finding home.'

Emma's face lit up. 'You should come to story time. Dad reads to kids on Saturday mornings, but grown-ups can come too. It's really good. Dad does different voices and everything.'

'Emma—'

'What?' Emma looked at her father innocently. 'She'd like it. And we need more people. It's only me and the little kids usually.'

Hugh met Joanna's eyes over his daughter's head. There was apology in his expression, but something else too. 'You'd be very welcome. If you wanted. Saturday mornings, ten o'clock. It's just an hour. We read, have biscuits, and talk about the stories. Very casual.'

Say no, Joanna's fear whispered. Too many people. Too much.

But she thought about the sunrise that morning. About choosing to walk through doors.

'Maybe,' she heard herself say. 'I'll think about it.'

'Brilliant!' Emma beamed. 'We'll see you Saturday then.'

She disappeared back into the back room before Joanna could correct her, leaving them alone again.

'Sorry about that,' Hugh said. 'She's... enthusiastic.'

'She's lovely.' Joanna meant it. 'She reminds me of myself at that age. Before...' She stopped. Couldn't finish.

'Before life happened?' Hugh suggested gently.

'Yes.'

They stood there a moment longer, and Joanna felt the pull again. The dangerous pull towards this man who understood, who'd been broken too, who looked at her like she mattered.

She stepped back. 'I should go. How much for the book?'

'Same as last time. Seven fifty.'

She paid, he wrapped the book, and this time when their fingers touched, she didn't pull back quite so quickly.

'Saturday,' Hugh said. 'No pressure. But the invitation stands.'

Joanna nodded and fled before she could make any promises she wasn't ready to keep.

##

That night, after reading three chapters of *The Shell Seekers* and feeling something in her heart grow with each page, Joanna sat in the conservatory and watched frost form on the glass.

The amaryllis was taller still. The bud was the size of her fist, green striped with deep red. Tomorrow, maybe. Tomorrow it would bloom.

And on the glass, in the frost patterns that formed and reformed as she watched, words appeared. Just for a moment, clear and unmistakable:

Trust.

Joanna reached out and touched the glass. It was warm under her fingers, impossibly warm, and the word lingered a moment longer before fading.

'I'm trying,' she whispered to the cottage. 'I'm really trying.'

The conservatory's warmth pulsed once, gently, like a heartbeat.

And outside, in the darkness, snow began to fall again—soft, quiet, covering the tracks she'd left on her walk up the hill, making everything new again.

Chapter Six

Friday morning, Joanna woke before dawn again and went up the hill.

This time it was easier. Her legs remembered the path, her lungs didn't burn quite so badly, and she reached the copse of pines just as the first light touched the eastern sky. She sat on the same fallen log and watched the sun rise over the Cotswolds, painting everything gold.

Her robin came again. As it sang its territorial song from a branch overhead, Joanna hummed along under her breath, feeling slightly mad but not caring.

When she got back to the cottage, pink-cheeked and clearheaded, she made tea and sat in the conservatory. The amaryllis bud was enormous now, the green skin splitting to reveal deep red petals beneath. Soon. Very soon.

She was halfway through her second cup when the knock came.

Mrs Willoughby stood on the doorstep

again, but this time she wasn't alone. Vivian and Dimity were with her—the couple Joanna had watched from her window with such longing.

Up close, they were striking together. Vivian was tall and broad-shouldered, dark hair showing threads of silver at the temples, grey-green eyes warm behind wire-rimmed glasses. He had a quiet, steady presence, the kind of man who would listen more than he spoke. He wore a thick jumper and corduroys, practical but well-made.

Dimity was petite and dark-haired, bundled in that same purple coat Joanna had seen from the window, her face open and kind. Her dark hair was pulled back in a simple ponytail, and her eyes sparkled with intelligence and warmth.

'Good morning, dear,' Mrs Willoughby said cheerfully. 'I've brought reinforcements. And bulbs.'

She held up a wooden trug filled with what looked like small brown onions.

'Bulbs?' Joanna repeated, confused.

'For the conservatory.' Mrs Willoughby sailed past her into the cottage as if she owned it. 'Spring bulbs—snowdrops, crocuses, early daffodils. They'll bloom even now, in winter, if we plant them in the conservatory. The cottage will see to it.'

Vivian and Dimity followed, both smiling at Joanna's bewildered expression.

'Don't fight it,' Vivian said in a cut-glass accent that suggested expensive schools and country estates. 'Mrs Willoughby has decided you need bulbs, so you're getting bulbs. Just go with it.'

'Much easier that way,' Dimity agreed. There was a lilt to her voice—Australian, Joanna thought—warm and open. 'And she's usually right.'

Before Joanna could protest, they'd taken over her kitchen. Mrs Willoughby was filling the kettle, Dimity was producing biscuits from somewhere, and Vivian was examining the conservatory with an approving eye.

'Oh, this is perfect,' Vivian called. 'Absolutely perfect. Look at that amaryllis! It's nearly ready to bloom.'

They all crowded into the small conservatory, cooing over the amaryllis like it was a newborn baby. And perhaps to the cottage it was—new life in the depths of winter, defying nature.

'Right,' Mrs Willoughby said decisively. 'Tea first, then planting. Joanna, dear, sit down. You look like you're about to bolt.'

Joanna sat, wide-eyed. She didn't know what else to do.

Over tea and biscuits, they asked Joanna questions but didn't push when she gave short answers. Where was she from? London, originally. What had brought her here? Family circumstances. Was she staying long? She didn't know.

'The cottage will tell you when it's time to go,' Mrs Willoughby said matter-of-factly. 'Or when it's time to stay. Whichever you need.'

After tea, they moved to the conservatory with the bulbs and a bag of potting soil that Mrs Willoughby had also somehow produced. She handed Joanna a terracotta pot and a trowel.

'Right. Fill the pot about halfway with soil.'

Joanna did as she was told. The soil was dark and rich, smelling of earth and growing things. When she plunged her hands into it, her spirits lifted. She couldn't remember the last time she'd touched soil. Years. Maybe decades.

'Good,' Mrs Willoughby said. 'Now the

bulbs. Pointy end up. Close together, they like company.'

Joanna arranged six small bulbs in the pot, covered them with more soil, and pressed it down gently. Her hands were dirty, soil under her fingernails, and it felt right. Felt like something she'd forgotten she knew how to do.

They planted pot after pot, which appeared in the conservatory as if by magic.

Magic! Joanne chuckled as she worked. Snowdrops, crocuses, miniature daffodils. The conservatory windowsills were filled with terracotta pots, and the cottage's warmth seemed to intensify.

'You have a gift for this,' Vivian observed, watching Joanna work. 'Have you gardened before?'

'My mother loved gardening.' The words came without thinking. 'When I was young, before... before she got ill. We had a garden. Nothing fancy, just a small patch behind the house. But she grew vegetables, herbs, and flowers. I helped her.'

'And after she got ill?' Mrs Willoughby asked gently.

'After, I looked after her. And then my

father. There wasn't time for gardens.' Joanna pressed soil around another bulb, focusing on her hands because that was easier than looking up. 'There wasn't time for anything except looking after them.'

The conservatory was quiet except for the sound of their hands in the soil, the gentle scrape of trowels against terracotta.

'How long did you care for them?' Dimity asked quietly.

'Ten years. Mum had dementia. Dad had a stroke three years after her diagnosis. By the end, they were both...' She couldn't finish. Didn't need to.

'That's a long time to put yourself aside,' Vivian said.

'I didn't mind. They needed me. I was useful.' Joanna laughed, but it came out wrong. 'That's what I'm good at. Being useful. Being needed. My husband used to say I was the most reliable person he'd ever met. Right up until he left.'

She hadn't meant to say that. But the words kept coming, like a dam breaking.

'Marcus. His name was Marcus. He left me ten years ago for his secretary—God, such a cliché—and I moved in with Mum the next week. So at least I was useful to someone, even if I wasn't enough for him. And now they're both gone, and I don't know who I am anymore. I don't know what I'm for.'

Her voice cracked on the last word. She stared at her soil-covered hands and felt tears slip down her cheeks.

A warm hand covered hers. Mrs Willoughby, kneeling beside her, squeezed gently.

'You're Joanna,' she said firmly. 'That's enough, dear. That's more than enough. The rest will come.'

'But what if it doesn't?' The question burst out of her. 'What if this is all I am? What if I've forgotten how to be anything else?'

'Then you'll remember,' Dimity said. She'd moved to Joanna's other side, her presence oddly comforting. 'One day at a time. One bulb at a time. You're already remembering, can't you feel it?'

And Joanna could. Her hands in the soil, planting things that would grow and bloom. Going up the hill to watch the sunrise. Reading books again. Walking into that bookshop, talking to Hugh, and almost agreeing to story time tomorrow.

Small things. But they were hers.

'The cottage knows,' Dimity added. 'It wouldn't have called you here if you weren't ready to heal.'

'But I don't feel ready,' Joanna whispered.

'Nobody ever does,' Mrs Willoughby said. 'But you're doing it anyway. That's what bravery looks like, dear. Not the absence of fear. Just doing the thing despite it.'

They sat there in the warm conservatory, surrounded by pots of bulbs that would bloom impossibly soon, and Joanna let herself cry properly for the first time since arriving. Not the broken sobs from before, but cleansing tears that felt like release.

When she finally stopped, Vivian handed her a handkerchief—actual linen, monogrammed. Dimity squeezed her shoulder, and Mrs Willoughby smiled as if Joanna had just done something wonderfully right.

'Better?' Mrs Willoughby asked.

'Yes.' Joanna wiped her eyes, managed a watery smile. 'Sorry. I didn't mean to fall apart.'

'Sometimes falling apart is necessary before we can put ourselves back together properly,' Vivian said. 'Believe me, I know.'

'We all do,' Dimity added. 'This village heals. We learned that very quickly.' The look she gave Vivian glowed with love.'

They finished planting the bulbs, washed their hands at the kitchen sink, and had more tea. The conversation moved to lighter things—village gossip, the upcoming Imbolc celebration, and whether the snow would hold for another week.

As they were leaving, Mrs Willoughby turned at the door.

'Story time tomorrow, yes? At the bookshop?'

Joanna hesitated. 'I'm not sure—'

'Emma will be so disappointed if you don't come,' Dimity said. 'She's told everyone in the village about the nice lady who's staying at Hawthorn Cottage.'

'Everyone?' Joanna's voice went up an octave.

'Small village,' Vivian said with a smile. 'You're the most exciting thing to happen since Dimity arrived. Embrace it.'

After they left, Joanna stood in the conservatory looking at all the newly planted bulbs. Twelve pots, arranged on the windowsills, soil dark and damp. Impossible that they'd bloom. But then, everything about this cottage was impossible.

The amaryllis bud had swollen even more. The green skin was splitting properly now, revealing deep crimson petals curled tight within. Tomorrow, she thought. Tomorrow it would open.

Tomorrow. Story time. Hugh. Emma. A roomful of people.

She could do this. She could walk through the door.

Maybe.

Saturday morning arrived too quickly.

Joanna woke to find the amaryllis in full bloom. Three enormous flowers on the thick stalk, blood-red and impossibly beautiful, their throats streaked with white. They filled the conservatory with their presence, dramatic and alive.

She sat in her chair and stared at them. The cottage had made them bloom overnight.

Magic. Real, undeniable magic.

If the cottage could make flowers bloom in winter, maybe it could help her bloom too.

That thought carried her through breakfast, through washing and dressing, through putting on her coat at nine thirty, even though story time wasn't until ten. She needed the extra time to talk herself out of changing her mind.

The walk to the bookshop took five minutes. Joanna stretched it to fifteen, walking slowly, stopping to watch the millstream, looking up at the hill where she'd watched two sunrises.

By the time she reached Chapter & Verse, it was five to ten, and she was almost hyperventilating.

Through the bow window, she could see people gathering. Children, mostly, sitting cross-legged on cushions arranged in a semicircle. Parents stood at the back, chatting. Hugh was there, arranging a chair, a book in his hand. Emma was helping him, moving cushions, laughing at something he said.

They looked happy. Complete. They didn't need her disrupting their Saturday morning.

Joanna turned to leave.

The bookshop door opened. A woman came

out with a toddler, smiled at Joanna. 'Going in? Story time's just starting. Hugh's brilliant—you won't regret it.'

She held the door open expectantly.

Joanna had no choice. She went inside.

The bell chimed. Every head turned. Joanna froze in the doorway, face burning, wanting desperately to run.

Then Emma saw her.

'You came!' The girl's face lit up like sunrise. She jumped up from her cushion and ran over, grabbed Joanna's hand. 'I saved you a spot. Come on, we're reading *The Lion, the Witch and the Wardrobe* today. It's brilliant.'

Before Joanna could protest, she was being towed to the back of the semicircle, pressed down onto a cushion between Emma and the wall. Safe. Hidden. She could slip out if she needed to.

Hugh had seen her. Their eyes met across the room, and his smile could have warmed winter itself.

'Right,' he said, his voice quiet but carrying. 'Shall we begin?'

He sat in the chair and opened the book, and when he started to read, his voice changed.

Became richer, more expressive. He did different voices for each character—Lucy's high sweetness, Edmund's sullenness, the Professor's absent-minded kindness. The children leaned forward, rapt. Even the parents stopped chatting to listen.

Joanna found herself leaning forward, too.

He read about Lucy stepping through the wardrobe into Narnia, about snow and lampposts and a faun with an umbrella. About a world that was always winter but never Christmas, until the right people arrived to change it.

Joanna's throat went tight. Always winter. She knew about that.

Hugh read for forty minutes straight, only stopping occasionally to show illustrations or ask the children questions. He was good at this. Patient, warm, genuinely engaged. Emma sat beside him, following along in her own copy, mouthing the words she knew by heart.

When he finally closed the book—stopping at a cliffhanger, of course—the children groaned in unison.

'Next week,' Hugh promised. 'Same time. And Mrs Pemberton's bringing biscuits.'

The children scattered. Parents collected them. The bookshop slowly emptied until it was just Hugh, Emma, and Joanna, who was still sitting on her cushion because her legs had forgotten how to work.

Emma bounced over. 'What did you think? Wasn't it good?'

'It was wonderful,' Joanna managed. Her voice sounded strange. 'Your dad's a very good reader.'

'He's the best.' Emma's pride was obvious. She looked at her father. 'Dad, Joanna liked it.'

Hugh came over and offered Joanna his hand to help her up. She took it, and the touch sent that same electricity up her arm. His hand was warm and gentle, and he held on just a moment longer than necessary.

'I'm so glad you came,' he said quietly.

'Me too,' Joanna said, and meant it.

Emma looked between them, a considering expression on her face that was far too knowing for twelve years old. 'Are you coming next week?'

'I...' Joanna looked at Hugh. His grey-blue eyes were hopeful, vulnerable. 'I'd like to.'

'Same time next week then?' Hugh asked.

Joanna nodded before fear could change her mind. 'Same time next week.'

Emma cheered. Hugh smiled. And Joanna's emotion unfolded, like the amaryllis opening its petals to the light.

Maybe, just maybe, her winter was ending, too.

Chapter Seven

The week that followed felt different.

Joanna went up the hill every morning to watch the sunrise. Monday, Tuesday, Wednesday, Thursday, Friday—five dawns in a row, each one beautiful in its own way. Her legs grew stronger. The path became familiar. And each morning when she came back to Hawthorn Cottage, pink-cheeked and clear-headed, the cottage seemed pleased with her.

The bulbs Mrs Willoughby had brought were growing. Fast, green shoots pushing up through the soil, reaching for the conservatory's constant warmth. By Wednesday, the first snowdrops had unfurled—delicate white bells that shouldn't bloom in January but did anyway. By Friday, the crocuses were showing colour, purple and gold and white.

Magic. All of it magic.

Joanna read *The Shell Seekers* curled in her chair, and the story wrapped around her heart. A woman looking back over her life, finding peace, understanding that the choices she'd made—even the painful ones—had led her to where she needed to be.

She wondered if she'd ever feel that way about her own choices. About Marcus, about the years of caregiving, about ending up here in this magic cottage with nothing but a battered suitcase and three hundred and forty-seven pounds in the bank.

Saturday morning came. Story time again.

This time, Joanna didn't hesitate. She woke, dressed, made tea, and walked to Chapter & Verse, arriving at exactly ten o'clock. The children were already gathering, Emma waving frantically from her spot near the front.

'You're here!' Emma beamed as Joanna settled onto the cushion beside her. 'I knew you'd come back.'

'You did?' Joanna asked.

'Of course. Dad said you would, too. He was right.'

Hugh was arranging his chair, book in hand, but he glanced up, and their eyes met. The smile he gave her was warm and slightly shy, and it made Joanna's insides tremble.

He read more of *The Lion, the Witch and the*

Wardrobe—the White Witch appearing, Edmund's betrayal, the arrival of Father Christmas, finally breaking the spell of endless winter. The children were enthralled. So was Joanna.

When he finished and the children scattered, Hugh came over to where Joanna was helping Emma stack cushions.

'You came back,' he said quietly.

'I said I would.'

'People say lots of things.' There was something in his voice, some old hurt, but it passed quickly. 'I'm pleased you meant it.'

Emma finished stacking the last cushion and turned to them with that too-knowing look again. 'Dad, you should ask Joanna if she wants coffee. There's that café across the square. They do good coffee. And cake.'

'Emma—' Hugh's ears went red.

'What? You said you wanted to talk to her properly. This is proper talking.' Emma looked at Joanna. 'He's too shy to ask. But he wants to. I can tell.'

'I'm standing right here,' Hugh said, but he was smiling despite his embarrassment. He looked at Joanna. 'She's not wrong, though.

Would you like coffee? The café across the square. Just coffee. And maybe cake, if Emma's recommendation counts for anything.'

Joanna's heart hammered. This was different from story time. This was deliberate. This was choosing to spend time together, just the two of them.

Say yes, something whispered. The cottage, maybe. Or maybe her

'I'd like that,' she said.

Emma's grin was triumphant. 'Brilliant. I'll go to Gran's. She's making lunch anyway. You two go and have a proper grown-up talk.'

She grabbed her coat and was gone before either of them could protest, the bell chiming her exit.

Hugh and Joanna looked at each other.

'I apologise for my daughter,' Hugh said. 'She's become very invested in my social life. Or lack thereof.'

'She's lovely,' Joanna said. 'She reminds me of myself at that age. Before I learned to be afraid of everything.'

'You're not afraid now.' Hugh's voice was gentle. 'You're here, aren't you?'

'Terrified, actually,' Joanna admitted. 'But

doing it anyway.'

'That's the definition of brave.' He held out his hand. Not to shake, just offering. 'Shall we?'

Joanna took his hand. His fingers closed around hers, warm and careful, and they walked out of the bookshop together.

##

The café was called The Cosy Cup, which was a bit twee, but somehow perfect. It was warm inside, the windows were misted up, and the air was rich with the aroma of brewing coffee and baking. A dozen small tables with mismatched chairs filled the small space with bunting strung across the ceiling, and watercolours of the village on the walls. Only a few tables were occupied—an elderly couple sharing a pot of tea, two women deep in conversation over laptops.

Hugh chose a table by the window overlooking the village green. He helped Joanna with her coat, pulled out her chair, and was so gentlemanly that she felt seventeen instead of fifty-one.

A woman appeared—middle-aged, cheerful, wearing an apron dusted with flour. 'Hugh!

Lovely to see you. And this must be Joanna from Hawthorn Cottage. Emma's been telling us all about you.'

'Has she?' Joanna managed a smile despite the heat creeping up her neck. 'I'm becoming quite well-known, it seems.'

'Small village,' the woman said, exactly as Vivian had. 'I'm Margaret, and The Cosy Cup is mine. What can I get you?'

They ordered coffee and, at Margaret's insistence, slices of the Victoria sponge in the display cabinet that she promised was fresh from the oven. When she bustled away, Joanna looked at Hugh.

'Does everyone in this village know everything about everyone?'

'Usually before it happens,' Hugh said with a smile. 'You get used to it. It's intrusive but also... heartening, in a way. Knowing people notice. Knowing people care.'

'I'm not sure I'm ready to be noticed.'

'You already are, I'm afraid. A woman staying at one of the magic cottages, going up the hill at dawn every day, coming to our story time—you're the most interesting thing to happen in the village since Dimity arrived.

Joanna frowned. 'You said cottages? Is the magic in many of them?'

Hugh nodded. 'Three that we know of for certain. Hawthorn Cottage, where you're staying. Pippin's Nook next door, where Vivian and Dimity live—that's where Dimity's sight came back after her accident. And she and Vivian fell in love. And Rose Cottage, where Mrs Willoughby found peace after leaving her abusive marriage decades ago. I'm sure there are more, but those three...' He paused, choosing his words carefully. 'Those three seem to call to people who need them most.'

'And everyone just... accepts this? That cottages can be magical?'

'We've seen it too many times not to,' Hugh said simply. 'People arrive broken. The cottages help them heal. Not always in obvious ways, not always quickly, but it happens. Enough that we don't question it anymore.'

'How do you know I go up the hill at dawn?' Joanna asked, still processing.

'Mrs Willoughby mentioned it. Who heard from someone who was up early walking their dog. Who saw you on the path.' Hugh's expression was rueful. 'Sorry. That's village life. But nobody means any harm. They're just... interested. Hopeful, even.'

'Hopeful?'

'That the cottage will help you. That you'll stay. That you'll become part of things.' He paused. 'The village likes healing people. Makes it feel useful, I think.'

Joanna stood there, absorbing this, and realised with a start that she wasn't questioning the magic at all. Wasn't arguing or dismissing it as impossible. She was talking about enchanted cottages as though they were something perfectly ordinary—like the weather or the church bells or the price of milk. When had that happened? When had she stopped needing rational explanations and started simply accepting that some things in this village defied logic?

Maybe the magic was already working on her, changing her in ways she hadn't noticed yet.

Margaret returned with their coffee and enormous slices of sponge. She left them to it with a knowing look that made Hugh's ears go red again.

Joanna looked down and hid her smile. She

took a bite of cake and nearly moaned. It was perfect—light sponge, sweet strawberry jam, and fresh cream. The kind of cake that reminded her of being a child and how uncomplicated those years had been.

'Good?' Hugh asked.

'Incredible.' She took another bite. 'I haven't had proper cake in... Gosh, I can't remember.'

'Margaret's a treasure. This place is her life's work. She opened it five years ago after her husband died. Said she needed something to fill her days, something to make people happy.'

'Healing herself by healing others,' Joanna said quietly.

'Exactly.' Hugh stirred his coffee, looked at her over the rim of his cup. 'Is that what you're doing? With the cottage?'

'I don't know what I'm doing,' Joanna admitted. 'I just know I couldn't stay where I was anymore. London, I mean. In my flat. Alone with... everything.'

'What's everything?'

She should have made something up, kept it light. But the cottage had been teaching her to be honest, and Hugh's grey-blue eyes were patient and kind, and the words came out before she could stop them.

'My husband left me ten years ago. For his secretary. I know, terribly clichéd. And I was... I was devastated. I didn't see it coming, which seems stupid now because of course, I should have seen it. We hadn't been happy in years. But I thought we were fine. I thought fine was enough.'

She took a breath. Hugh waited, didn't fill the silence.

'My mother was diagnosed with dementia the same month Marcus left. So, I moved in with her and became her carer; my father was still at work. Then he had a stroke three years later, and I looked after him too. Ten years of it all together. Hospitals and prescriptions and appointments and watching my parents both slowly disappear.' Her voice cracked, but she kept going. 'They died within months of each other. Last year. And suddenly I was free, except I didn't know how to be free anymore. I'd forgotten how to be anything except useful. Except needed. And nobody needed me anymore, and I really didn't know what to do with myself.'

She looked down at her cake, half-eaten. 'Sorry. That's rather a lot to dump on someone over coffee.'

'Don't apologise.' Hugh's voice was rough. 'I understand. More than you could know.'

He was quiet for a moment, stirring his spoon even though the cup was empty. 'Sarah died four years ago. My wife. Cancer. We had eighteen months from diagnosis to... the end. Eighteen months of treatments and false hopes, and her getting weaker and weaker until she was barely there anymore.'

Joanna reached across the table without thinking, covered his hand with hers.

Hugh looked at their joined hands, then at her. 'Emma was eight. She was so small, and she had to watch her mother die slowly, and there was nothing I could do to protect her from it. Nothing except be there, day after day, watching Sarah slip away.'

'I'm so sorry,' Joanna whispered.

'Towards the end, I used to think... I used to wish it would be over. Not just for Sarah's sake, but for mine. For Emma's. I was so tired. So exhausted. And I'd think, please, just let this end. Let her go so we can start healing.'

His voice broke. 'And then she did go, and the guilt was crushing. Because I'd wished for it. I'd wanted my wife to die so I could stop being tired.'

'Hugh, no.' Joanna squeezed his hand. 'That's not what you wanted. You wanted her suffering to end. That's not the same thing.'

'Isn't it?'

'No. It's human. It's what anyone would feel.' She knew about this, about the complicated tangle of love and exhaustion and relief and guilt. 'I felt the same way with my parents. Especially towards the end with Dad. I'd think, please just let him go. Let us both be free. And then when he died, I felt so guilty I could barely breathe.'

They sat there, hands joined across the table, two broken people trying to convince each other they weren't so selfish after all.

'How do you live with it?' Hugh asked finally. 'The guilt?'

'I don't know yet. I'm still working on it.' Joanna managed a small smile. 'The cottage is helping. This village. The sunrise walks. Story time.' She held his eyes, and couldn't believe her boldness. 'You.'

'Me?'

'Knowing someone else understands. That I'm not... that I'm not the only one who feels this way.' She looked at their joined hands. 'That helps more than you might think.'

Hugh turned his hand over, threaded his fingers through hers properly. The gesture was intimate, deliberate, and warmth spread up Joanna's arm and into her chest.

'I haven't talked to anyone about Sarah like this,' he said quietly. 'Not in four years. Emma's too young to be burdened with it, and my mother tries, but she doesn't really understand. She thinks I should be over it by now. That four years is long enough.'

'There's no such thing as long enough,' Joanna said. 'Grief doesn't have a timeline.'

'No. But guilt does, apparently. I'm supposed to have forgiven myself by now. Moved on. Been happy.' He laughed, but it held bitterness. 'Sarah even told me to, towards the end, when she was lucid one last time. She said, "Promise me you'll be happy. Promise me you'll live." And I promised. And I've spent four years feeling guilty for not keeping that promise.'

'Maybe you're starting to keep it now,' Joanna suggested. 'Maybe that's what this is.'

'This?'

She gestured between them. At their joined hands, at the café around them, at the conversation that had stripped them both bare. 'This. Talking. Connecting. Letting yourself want something again.'

Hugh's eyes went very serious. 'Is that what you're doing? Letting yourself want things again?'

Joanna's heart hammered. 'I'm trying to. The cottage is teaching me. One small thing at a time. Sunrise walks. Reading books. Story time. Coffee with...'

She couldn't finish. Couldn't say with you out loud because that felt too big, too dangerous.

But Hugh smiled. 'Coffee with me.'

'Yes.' The word came out as barely a whisper.

They sat there, hands joined, looking at each other across the table. Outside, snow had started falling again, soft flakes drifting past the window. The café was warm, the cake was sweet, and for the first time in ten years, Joanna felt something unfamiliar: happiness.

Not complete happiness. Not uncomplicated happiness. But the beginning of it. The possibility of something to grow.

Hugh's thumb traced circles on her palm, probably without him even realising. His touch was gentle, rhythmic, and calming.

'I should tell you,' he said quietly, 'that I haven't done this in four years. Coffee with a woman. Talking like this. Wanting...'

He stopped. Started again.

'When you walked into my shop that first time, I felt something I thought was dead. And it terrified me. Because Sarah's only been gone four years, and what kind of person moves on that quickly?'

'A person who's lonely and brave enough to admit it,' Joanna said quietly.

'You think I'm brave?'

'I think we both are. We're here, aren't we? Holding hands in a café, telling each other terrible truths. That takes real courage.'

Hugh laughed, and this time it was real. 'God, we're a pair, aren't we? We're so broken we can barely function. What are we doing?'

'Healing?' Joanna suggested. 'Or trying to.

Together, maybe.'

'Together,' Hugh repeated. His grip on her hand tightened. 'I like the sound of that.'

They finished their coffee, ate their cake, and talked about lighter things. Books they loved. Places they'd lived. Emma's school, how she was doing, and how proud Hugh was of her resilience. Joanna's writing—she admitted she'd always wanted to try it but never had time—and Hugh immediately insisted she should, that the cottage would probably help with that too.

By the time they left, an hour had passed, and Joanna's cheeks ached from smiling.

Hugh walked her home. They crossed the green together, his hand hovering near her elbow but not quite touching. The snow fell around them, soft and quiet, and the village looked like something from a storybook.

At her gate, they stopped. Hawthorn Cottage glowed behind them, warm light in the windows, smoke rising from the chimney. Welcoming her home.

'Thank you,' Joanna said. 'For coffee. For talking. For... everything.'

'Thank you for saying yes.' Hugh smiled,

and he looked younger when he did. Less burdened. 'Would you... could I see you again? Properly, I mean. Not just at story time.'

'I'd like that,' Joanna said. And then, because the cottage had been teaching her to be brave, she said, 'I'd like that very much.'

Hugh's smile widened. He reached out, tucked a strand of hair behind her ear, and the touch sent electricity through her. For a moment, she thought he might kiss her. She wanted him to kiss her with an intensity that shocked her.

But he just smiled and stepped back.

'Next week?' he asked.

'Next week,' Joanna agreed.

She watched him walk away across the green, hands in his pockets, occasionally looking back. When he turned the corner by the bookshop, she went inside.

The cottage wrapped her in warmth immediately. The fire crackled approval. The conservatory glowed, and when Joanna went to check on the bulbs, she found three crocuses had opened fully—purple and gold and white, absolutely beautiful.

And on the conservatory glass, written in

condensation that shouldn't exist were the words, **Well done.**

Joanna laughed and touched the words. They faded under her fingers, but the warmth remained.

Outside, snow kept falling. The village settled into its Saturday afternoon. And Joanna sat in her chair with her heart full and her hands still tingling from where Hugh had held them, and thought, maybe she could heal.

Maybe they both could.

Chapter Eight

In the days that followed, Joanne began to feel she was living in a different world.

She went up the hill every morning, but now, when she stood at the summit watching the sunrise, she wasn't just thinking about her own healing. She was thinking about Hugh. About the way his hand had felt holding hers. About the circles his thumb had traced on her palm. About how he'd looked at her across that table as if she mattered.

It was terrifying.

She tried to read *The Shell Seekers* but kept rereading the same paragraphs, her mind wandering to grey-blue eyes and kind smiles. The conservatory was a riot of blooms now—snowdrops and crocuses and the first brave daffodils pushing up through the soil—and every time she looked at them, she thought about growth and risk and the danger of opening yourself up to something that could hurt you.

Because it would hurt. Eventually. She knew that with a bone-deep certainty that ten years of loneliness had taught her. People left. People stopped loving you. People found someone better, someone easier, someone who wasn't so broken and complicated and afraid.

But she went to story time on Saturday anyway.

Hugh read more of *The Lion, the Witch and the Wardrobe*—Aslan appearing, the stone table, the moment when winter finally breaks and spring floods back into Narnia. The children cheered. Emma beamed. And when Hugh closed the book, he looked directly at Joanna with an expression that made her breath catch.

Afterwards, when the children had scattered, and Emma had conveniently remembered she needed to help Mrs Willoughby with something urgent, Hugh walked Joanna home.

They talked about books, about the village, about nothing important. But his hand brushed hers three times as they walked, and the third time, he caught her fingers and held on. Just like that. As if it were the most natural thing in the world.

'I've been thinking about you,' he said as they reached her gate.

Joanna's heart hammered. 'Have you?'

'Constantly. Probably more than is healthy.' He smiled, self-deprecating. 'Emma says I'm distracted. She's right. I burned dinner twice this week because I was thinking about... well. About you.'

'I've been thinking about you too,' Joanna admitted. 'Also, probably more than is healthy.'

They stood there at the gate, snow falling around them, and the moment stretched tight with possibility.

'Would you like to come for Sunday lunch tomorrow?' Hugh asked. 'Just us. Well, us and Emma. Nothing fancy. Just roast chicken and conversation. If you're comfortable with that.'

Say no, fear whispered. Too fast. Too much. Too dangerous.

But Joanna had been learning to ignore fear.

'I'd love to,' she said.

##

Sunday lunch at Hugh's house was both wonderful and overwhelming.

He lived above the bookshop in a flat that was cosy and cluttered, and full of books. Every surface held them—shelves, tables, stacked on the floor. The kitchen was tiny but warm, smelling of roasting chicken and herbs. Emma had set the table with what was clearly the good china, and she'd even put a small vase with snowdrops at the centre of the table.

'From our garden,' she explained proudly. 'Well, Gran's garden. But I picked them.'

They were the same snowdrops that grew in Joanna's conservatory. Magic recognising magic.

Lunch was easy. Hugh cooked while Emma chattered about school and books and the village, filling any silences with her bright liveliness. Joanna found herself relaxing despite her nerves, laughing at Emma's stories, and then helping Hugh with the dishes while Emma disappeared to her room to find a book she wanted to show Joanna.

And then it was just the two of them in the small kitchen, standing close because there wasn't much room, and Hugh turned to her with a tea towel in his hands and said, 'I'm really glad you came.'

'So am I,' Joanna said.

'Joanna, I—' He stopped, started again. 'I

need to be honest with you. About what I'm feeling. Because I'm not good at this, at dating or whatever this is, and I don't want to mess it up by not being clear.'

Her heart stuttered. 'All right.'

'I like you. More than like you, if I'm being honest. And I know it's only been a few weeks, and I know we're both complicated and damaged and probably terrible candidates for any kind of relationship. But I can't stop thinking about you. Can't stop wanting to see you, talk to you, be near you.'

He set down the tea towel, took a step closer.

'And I keep thinking that Sarah would want this for me. She'd want me to be happy. And I know she'd be cross with me for feeling guilty about it. But knowing that doesn't make the guilt go away.'

Joanna reached up and touched his cheek. The gesture surprised them both. 'I understand. I feel the same way. Wanting, but the fear and the guilt… Plus the certainty that I'm going to mess this up somehow.'

'What if we mess it up together?' Hugh asked. His hand came up to cover hers, holding it against his face. 'What if we just... try? And see what happens?'

'I'm terrified,' Joanna whispered.

'Me too.' He smiled. 'But I'm more terrified of not trying. Of letting fear keep me from something that will be wonderful.'

They stood there in the domesticity of the tiny kitchen, Hugh's hand on hers, Joanna's heart hammering so hard she was certain he could hear it. Emma's footsteps sounded overhead, and they both jumped apart like guilty teenagers.

Emma appeared a moment later with three books and a detailed explanation of why Joanna absolutely had to read them. The moment was broken, but the emotion remained, hovering between them like electricity.

When it was time to leave, Hugh walked her home again. At her door, in the gathering dusk with snow falling softly around them, he said, 'Can I see you this week? Properly, I mean. Maybe Wednesday evening? I could bring dinner. We could just... talk.'

'I'd like that,' Joanna said.

He leaned in. Slowly, giving her time to pull away. His hand came up to cup her cheek, and

Joanna's breath stopped completely.

This was it. He was going to kiss her. And she wanted it, wanted it with an intensity that shocked her.

His lips were an inch from hers when panic slammed into her chest like a fist. Marcus had kissed her like this once, gentle and promising, and look how that had ended. Ten years alone. Ten years of not being good enough.

I can't do this.

Joanna pulled back sharply, nearly stumbling. 'I'm sorry. I can't. I'm sorry.'

She fumbled for her keys, got the door open, and fled inside before Hugh could respond.

##

The cottage tried to comfort her.

Fire burning bright, warmth wrapping around her, the conservatory glowing with its impossible blooms. But Joanna paced the sitting room, hands shaking, heart racing, panic crawling up her throat.

What had she been thinking? Letting herself get close to Hugh, letting herself want things, letting herself hope? She was fifty-one years old with nothing to offer. No money, no prospects, no life beyond this borrowed cottage and borrowed time.

He deserved better. Emma deserved better. They were healing, moving forward, building a life. They didn't need her disrupting everything with her damage and her fear and her inability to trust.

She should leave. Before this went any further. Before she hurt them. Before they hurt her.

The thought crystallised into certainty.

Leave. Pack. Go. Before it's too late.

Joanna ran upstairs and dragged her suitcase from under the bed, and started throwing clothes into it with shaking hands. She didn't have much. She'd never unpacked completely anyway. She could be gone in twenty minutes.

Go where? a small voice asked.

Anywhere. London. Another town. It didn't matter. She'd figure something out. She always did.

Except she didn't, did she? She'd ended up here because she'd had nowhere else to go. No money, no plan, nothing except a distant cousin's charity.

But I can't stay.

She couldn't accept the cottage healing her

or accept the way Hugh looked at her with those hopeful eyes. She couldn't keep pretending she was someone capable of moving forward instead of someone permanently broken.

She zipped the suitcase, grabbed her coat, and went downstairs.

The cottage was quiet around her. Watchful. The fire had died down to embers, and the temperature had dropped noticeably.

Joanna ignored the sudden change. She grabbed her bag, her keys, and headed for the front door.

She put her hand on the handle and turned it.

Nothing happened.

She tried again, pulling harder. The handle moved, but the door stayed shut. Not locked—she'd unlocked it when she came in. Just... stuck.

'Come on,' she muttered, yanking. 'Come on, come on.'

The door wouldn't budge.

Joanna dropped her suitcase and tried with both hands, pulling with all her strength. Nothing. The door might as well have been welded shut.

'Please,' she said, and her voice broke.

'Please, just let me go.'

The cottage didn't answer, but the fire flared suddenly in the sitting room, bright and insistent.

'No!' Joanna shouted at it. 'I can't do this. I can't stay here and pretend I'm getting better when all I'm doing is setting myself up to be destroyed again. I can't let myself care about Hugh and Emma when I know how this ends. I can't!'

She yanked at the door again, sobbing now, desperate. But it wouldn't open. The cottage was keeping her here. Keeping her safe from herself.

'I'm not safe!' she screamed at the walls, at the fire, at the magic that thought it knew what was best for her. 'I'm broken! Don't you understand? I'm too broken to fix!'

The fire crackled. The conservatory's warmth reached towards her. And very gently, very firmly, the cottage held her in its care.

Joanna sank to the floor, her back against the immovable door, and wept. Great tearing sobs. She cried for Marcus leaving, for her parents dying, for ten years of being invisible and useful but never enough. She cried for

Hugh's kind eyes and Emma's bright smile and the future she was too afraid to reach for.

She cried until there was nothing left.

And when the tears finally stopped, when she was empty and wrung out and exhausted, she opened her eyes and saw what the cottage had done.

Every light was on. Every single one. The cottage was blazing with brightness, refusing to let her sit in darkness. The fire burned high and warm. And in the conservatory—she could see it from where she sat—every flower had opened. The amaryllis, the snowdrops, the crocuses, the daffodils. All of them turned towards her like small suns, blooming in defiance of winter, blooming because they could, because magic said they could, because growth was possible even when everything said it wasn't.

'I'm scared,' Joanna whispered to the cottage.

The warmth pulsed. Once. Twice. Like a heartbeat.

'What if he leaves? What if I'm not enough? What if I let myself love him and he realises I'm just... broken?'

The fire popped, sending up sparks. On the wall, shadows danced. And in the conservatory, one of the amaryllis flowers trembled, as if moved by a breeze that didn't exist.

Joanna pulled her knees to her chest and rested her forehead on them. 'I don't know how to do this. How to trust again. How to believe in good things.'

But she was still here. In the cottage. Still being held by a magic that refused to let her run away.

Maybe that was enough for tonight. Maybe tomorrow she could think about Hugh's face when she'd pulled away, about the hurt in his eyes. Maybe tomorrow she could work out how to apologise, how to explain to him. Maybe try again.

But tonight, she just sat on the floor in her cottage surrounded by enchanted flowers, and let the magic calm her. Outside, snow fell. The village slept. And Hawthorn Cottage blazed with light, holding Joanna together while she learned—slowly, painfully, one breath at a time—how to look forwards.

Chapter Nine

Joanna woke on the floor, stiff and cold and disoriented.

Grey dawn light filtered through the windows. The fire had died to ash. Her suitcase sat by the front door where she'd dropped it, accusatory and pathetic in equal measure.

She'd fallen asleep against the door. The door that wouldn't open. The cottage that had kept her prisoner for her own good.

Joanna stood slowly, joints protesting, and tried the handle again.

It opened easily.

Of course it did. The cottage had made its point. Magic had kept her safe through the worst of her panic and tears and the desperate need to run. Now it was morning, and she could leave if she really wanted to.

But did she want to?

Joanna stood in the open doorway, cold air rushing in, and looked out at the village. The green was pristine under fresh snow. Smoke rose from chimneys. The church spire pointed skyward, steadfast and eternal. The millstream ran cheerful and bright, its song never-ending.

Hugh was out there somewhere. In his flat above the bookshop, probably making breakfast for Emma, probably wondering why Joanna had fled from him last night like he'd done something wrong when all he'd done was try to kiss her.

She closed the door. Not because it forced her to, but because she chose to.

Joanna made tea with shaking hands and carried it to the conservatory. The flowers were still open, still turned towards where she'd sat last night. The amaryllis blooms were beginning to fade now—they'd been open for days, which was magic in itself, but then everything here was touched by magic. The snowdrops and crocuses were still perfect, still defiant, still proving that growth was possible even in the depths of winter.

She sat in her chair and cried again, but softly this time. Exhausted tears. Healing tears.

The knock came at nine o'clock.

Joanna had known it would. The cottage had a way of summoning Mrs Willoughby when she was needed.

She opened the door.

Mrs Willoughby stood on the doorstep with a basket and a knowing look. No surprise in her expression, just compassion and determination.

'My dear,' she said gently. 'I think we should talk.'

Joanna nodded, couldn't speak, and let her in.

##

They sat in the conservatory with tea and the scones Mrs Willoughby had brought—still warm, as always, as if she'd baked them specifically for this moment and maybe she had. Maybe the cottage had told her. Maybe the whole bloody village knew by now that Joanna had lost her mind last night and tried to run away.

'I am pathetic,' Joanna said finally, staring at her untouched scone. 'Completely pathetic. A grown woman having a breakdown because a sweet man tried to kiss her.'

'You're not pathetic.' Mrs Willoughby's voice was firm. 'You're frightened. There's a difference.'

'I hurt him. Hugh. I saw his face when I

pulled away. I hurt him, and Emma probably knows by now, and they'll both think I'm—'

'Scared,' Mrs Willoughby completed. 'Which you are. And Hugh Morrison, of all people, understands scared. Give him some credit, dear.'

Joanna picked at her scone, pulling it into crumbs. 'I tried to leave. Last night. Packed my bag, tried to go. The cottage wouldn't let me.'

'Good.'

'Good?' Joanna looked up sharply. 'I was a prisoner. The door wouldn't open.'

'The cottage was keeping you safe.' Mrs Willoughby poured more tea with steady hands. 'From yourself, primarily. You weren't ready to leave. You're still not ready. You were just frightened.'

'I'm always frightened.'

'Yes, but you're doing things anyway. That's rather the point.' Mrs Willoughby studied her over the rim of her cup. 'Now, tell me what you're really afraid of, dear. Not the surface fear. The deep one.'

Joanna's throat closed. She shook her head.

'Tell me,' Mrs Willoughby said, gentle but implacable.

The words came out in a rush. 'I'm afraid I'll let myself love him, and then he'll realise I'm nothing special. I'm just a broken middle-aged woman with no money and no prospects and too much baggage. That he'll get bored, or tired, or he'll meet someone better. Someone younger, someone easier, someone who doesn't sit on the floor and cry and try to run away when happiness gets too close.'

Tears rolled down her cheeks again 'I'm afraid I'll give Hugh everything I have left, and it won't be enough. It wasn't enough for Marcus. I gave Marcus thirteen years, and he still left. So, what makes me think I'd be enough for Hugh?'

Mrs Willoughby set down her cup and moved to sit beside Joanna, taking her hand. 'Oh, my dear. You're looking at this all wrong.'

'Am I?'

'Completely.' Mrs Willoughby squeezed her fingers. 'Marcus was a fool who didn't deserve you. That says nothing about your worth and everything about his character. But you've spent ten years believing his leaving was your fault, haven't you?'

Joanna nodded miserably.

'It wasn't. Marriages end for all sorts of reasons, but you being "not enough" wasn't one of them. You were enough. You are enough. Marcus was simply incapable of seeing it.'

'But what if—'

'What if Hugh is the same?' Mrs Willoughby finished. 'What if you open your heart and he breaks it? What if you try and fail? What if, what if, what if.' She shook her head. 'Joanna, you can't live your life in what-ifs. You'll suffocate under them.'

'But I don't know how to trust again,' Joanna whispered. 'How do you trust someone after you've been broken?'

Mrs Willoughby was quiet for a long moment. When she spoke, her voice was softer, more personal. 'I was married once. Did you know that?'

Joanna shook her head.

'A long, long time ago. Forty years, nearly. I was young and naive and desperately in love with a man who seemed perfect. He wasn't. He drank. He hit me twice before I finally left. I was twenty-five and terrified and certain I'd never trust anyone again.'

'Oh, Mrs Willoughby—'

'It's all right, dear. It was a lifetime ago.' Mrs Willoughby patted her hand. 'But I spent the next fifteen years alone. Absolutely convinced that trusting anyone would lead to pain. Built walls around myself so high that nothing could get through. I was safe. Lonely, but safe.'

She smiled, but it was sad. 'And then I came here. To our village. And slowly, so slowly, I barely noticed, those walls came down. People here—they didn't push. They just... kept showing up. Kept being kind. Kept proving that not everyone would hurt me.'

'How did you let them in?' Joanna asked.

'I chose to. That's all it was, really. A choice. Every day, sometimes every hour, I chose to trust just a little bit more. To believe that these people were different. That I was safe here.'

'And were you? Safe?'

'Yes.' Mrs Willoughby's smile warmed. 'I was. I am. But I had to choose it, Joanna. The magic here can open doors, but you have to walk through them. The cottage can heal you, but you have to let it. Hugh can offer you love, but you have to be brave enough to accept it.'

Joanna looked at their joined hands. Mrs Willoughby's age-spotted and strong, capable hands that had survived pain and come through it.

'What if I'm not brave enough?' Joanna whispered.

'Then you practise. Small steps. You've already taken so many—coming here, climbing that hill every morning, going to story time, having coffee with Hugh. Those were all choices. All brave choices.'

'Running away last night wasn't brave.'

'No, but staying was. You could have climbed out a window, you know. The cottage might have locked the door, but it didn't trap you completely. You could have left if you'd really wanted to.' Mrs Willoughby tilted her head. 'But you stayed. You let the cottage hold you. You chose to still be here this morning. That's brave, dear.'

Joanna looked up. 'I suppose.'

'Not suppose. Definitely.' Mrs Willoughby squeezed her hand once more and released it. 'Now. Let me ask you something, and I want you to answer honestly. Not what's safe or sensible or reasonable. What do you want,

Joanna? What do you really want?'

The question hung in the air between them.

What did she want?

Not what she should want. Not what was practical. What did she want?

'I want...' Joanna's voice shook. 'I want Hugh. I want to see if this thing between us could be real. I want to watch him read to those children every Saturday and have coffee with him and hold his hand and not be terrified every second that he's going to leave.'

'What else?'

'I want Emma. Not to replace her mother, I'd never presume that. But to be in her life somehow. To see her grow up. To be someone she can talk to.'

'What else?'

The words came faster now, spilling out. 'I want friends. Real friends, like Vivian and Dimity. Like you. I want to be part of this village, part of something bigger than myself. I want to wake up in this cottage every morning and not feel like I'm borrowing someone else's life. I want it to be mine. I want to stay.'

She stopped, breathless. The truth of it sat in her chest, huge and terrifying and absolutely certain.

'I want to stay,' she repeated, quieter. 'I don't want to leave. I want this to be home.'

Mrs Willoughby beamed. 'There. Was that so hard?'

'Yes,' Joanna said, but she was smiling through her tears. 'Bloody terrifying, actually.'

'But you said it. You admitted what you want. That's the first step, dear. Everything else follows from that.' Mrs Willoughby stood, brushed crumbs from her skirt. 'Now, to practical matters. Imbolc is in two weeks— February first. Do you know what that is?'

'No.'

'It's an ancient festival. The celebration of light returning, of winter beginning to break. The village has always marked it—bonfire, candles, blessings for the year ahead. We're having the planning meeting this Saturday at my cottage. I'd like you to come. Help with the organisation.'

'Me?' Joanna's voice went up. 'But I don't know anything about—'

'You don't need to know anything. You just need to be there. Be a part of it. Let yourself belong.' Mrs Willoughby fixed her with a stern look. 'And you need to talk to Hugh. Today. Explain what happened. Apologise and try again.'

'I don't know what to say to him.'

'The truth is usually a good start.' Mrs Willoughby headed for the door, then paused. 'He cares about you, dear. Quite a lot, if I'm any judge. And Hugh Morrison doesn't give his heart easily. If he's offering it to you, that means he sees something in you worth staying for. Worth loving. Believe him.'

'What if I break his heart?'

'What if he breaks yours?' Mrs Willoughby countered. 'What if, what if, what if. Stop living in what-ifs and start living in what-is. What is, is that a good man cares about you. What is, is that you care about him. What is, is that you have a chance at happiness if you're brave enough to reach for it.'

The elderly woman opened the door, letting in cold air and watery morning sunlight. 'Saturday, dear. Two o'clock. Rose Cottage. Don't make me send the cottage to drag you there.'

She left, and Joanna sat alone in the conservatory with the truth she'd finally admitted.

She wanted to stay. Wanted Hugh. Wanted all of it.

Now she just had to be brave enough to fight for it.

##

The cottage sighed around her.

Joanna felt it—a release of tension, a settling, as if the building itself had been holding its breath and could finally exhale. The temperature rose noticeably. The fire in the sitting room, which had been dead ash, suddenly crackled back to life.

In the conservatory, the flowers seemed to take on new life. The amaryllis, which had been drooping, straightened its blooms. And on the windowsill, the bulbs Mrs Willoughby had brought burst into sudden, riotous growth. In the space of a heartbeat, green shoots tripled in height, buds formed and swelled and opened. More snowdrops, more crocuses, and—impossibly—a scatter of tiny blue flowers Joanna didn't recognise but which smelled of honey and distant spring.

'All right,' she said to the cottage. 'All right. I get it. I'm staying. I'm trying. I'll talk to

Hugh. I'll go to the planning meeting. I'll... I'll be brave.'

The warmth pulsed. Approval, comfort, encouragement.

Joanna stood and went to the mirror in the hallway. Looked at herself properly for the first time in days. Her hair was a mess, her face blotchy from crying, her clothes rumpled from sleeping on the floor.

But her eyes were clearer than they'd been in years.

She looked like someone who'd survived a storm. Someone who'd broken and was putting herself back together. Someone who was healing, slowly, painfully, one choice at a time.

'Right,' she said to her reflection. 'Bath. Proper clothes. Then I'm going to talk to Hugh and grovel like mad and hope to God he doesn't slam the door in my face.'

Her reflection looked back, uncertain but determined.

Joanna went upstairs.

Behind her, the cottage hummed with contentment. The fire burned bright. The flowers bloomed. And on the conservatory glass, written in condensation that spelled itself out letter by letter, a single word appeared.

Brave.

Outside, the morning brightened. Snow melted in patches where the sun touched. A robin sang from the apple tree, loud and insistent. The village woke to Monday, ordinary and magical in equal measure.

And in Hawthorn Cottage, a woman who'd forgotten how to hope was healing.

Chapter Ten

Joanna had bathed, dressed in clean clothes, and brushed her hair until it behaved. She'd eaten a piece of toast she didn't taste, and drank tea that went cold while she stared at it. Three times she'd put her coat on, and taken it off twice before finally making herself walk out the door at eleven o'clock.

Monday morning. The shop would be open. Hugh would be there.

She had no idea what she was going to say.

The village was quiet as she stepped outside; most people were at work or tucked inside their cottages. The millstream ran its happy course, and Joanna focused on that sound as she walked—water flowing, persistent, unstoppable. Like time. Like healing.

Chapter & Verse looked warm through its bow windows. Joanna could see Hugh moving about inside, shelving books. Her heart hammered so hard her stomach twisted

She could turn around.

Come back later.

Tomorrow.

Next week.

Never.

But Mrs Willoughby's words echoed: *Stop living in what-ifs and start living in what-is.*

Joanna pushed open the door.

The bell chimed. Hugh looked up, and his expression did something complicated—surprise, hope, wariness, all flashing across his face in the space of a heartbeat.

'Joanna.' His voice was guarded. 'Hello.'

'Hello.' She stood just inside the door, hand still on the handle, ready to bolt. 'Is this a bad time?'

'No. It's fine. I'm just—' He gestured vaguely at the shelves. 'Restocking. Monday's usually our quiet day.'

An elderly woman emerged from the back of the shop with an armful of paperbacks, nodded pleasantly at Joanna, and went to the counter. Hugh excused himself, rang up her purchases, and made small talk about the weather. The whole time, Joanna stood frozen by the door, panic rising with each passing second.

This was a mistake. She should go. Should—

The woman left. The bell chimed. And then it was just the two of them in the quiet shop with the wood stove crackling and books surrounding them like witnesses.

'I'm sorry,' Joanna blurted. 'About last night. I'm so, so sorry.'

Hugh set down the books he'd been holding. 'You don't need to apologise.'

'I do. I absolutely do. You were kind and lovely, and you didn't do anything wrong, and I panicked and ran away like a child, and I'm mortified, and I completely understand if you never want to see me again, but I needed to at least explain—'

'Joanna.' Hugh's voice was gentle. 'Breathe.'

She breathed. Shaky and uneven, but she breathed.

'Can we sit?' Hugh gestured to the leather armchair by the stove. 'Please? I think we need to talk properly.'

Joanna nodded and followed him. He pulled over a second chair, so they faced each other, knees almost touching. Close but not crowding.

The fire crackled beside them.

'I'm sorry,' she said again, quieter this time.

'Stop apologising.' Hugh leaned forward, hands clasped between his knees. 'What happened last night—that wasn't about me doing something wrong, was it? That was about you being frightened.'

'Terrified,' Joanna admitted. 'Completely terrified. Of you, of this, of everything.'

'Of me?' Hugh's brow furrowed. 'Have I pushed too hard? Moved too fast? Because if I have—'

'No. God, no. You've been perfect. That's rather the problem.' Joanna twisted her hands in her lap. 'You're kind and patient and wonderful with Emma, and you look at me like I matter, and I don't know how to handle that. Because the last man who looked at me that way left me for someone else, and I can't... I can't survive that again.'

Hugh was quiet for a moment. Then: 'Your husband. Marcus.'

'Yes.' The name still hurt to say. 'We were married thirteen years. I thought we were fine. Not deliriously happy, maybe, but fine. Solid. And then one day he sat me down and told me he'd been having an affair with his secretary for eight months and he was leaving.'

Her voice cracked, but she kept going. 'He said he was sorry, but he'd been unhappy for years, and I must have known. But I didn't know. I didn't see it coming at all. Which means either I'm completely oblivious or I was so unimportant to him that he didn't think I'd notice.'

'Joanna—'

'And the worst part?' She looked up at Hugh, eyes burning. 'The absolute worst part is that after he left, I spent years wondering what was wrong with me. What I'd failed to do, what I'd failed to be, that made him look elsewhere. And I still don't have an answer. I was just... not enough.'

'That's not true,' Hugh said fiercely. 'That's not true at all. You were enough. He was the one who failed. Not you.'

'My mother said that. And Mrs Willoughby this morning. But it doesn't change how it feels. It doesn't change the fact that I gave him everything and it wasn't enough to make him stay.' She wiped at her eyes angrily. 'So, when you tried to kiss me last night, all I could think was: what happens when he realises I'm not enough either? What happens when he gets bored, or tired, or meets someone better? Because people leave, Hugh. People always leave.'

The silence stretched between them, heavy with old hurts.

Finally, Hugh spoke. 'I understand. More than you might think. Because I'm terrified too.'

'You are?'

He nodded. 'Sarah was the love of my life. I met her when I was twenty-five and married her at twenty-seven and thought we'd have fifty years together. We got eighteen. And watching her die—' His voice broke. 'It was the worst thing I've ever been through. Worse than anything I could have imagined.'

Joanna reached out, took his hand. He gripped it like a lifeline.

'And at the end, when she was barely conscious, she made me promise I'd be happy again. That I'd live. That I wouldn't waste years grieving her.' Hugh stared at their joined hands. 'I promised. And then she died, and I spent four years feeling guilty for being alive when she wasn't. For being exhausted instead of heartbroken all the time. For occasionally going whole hours without thinking about her.'

'Hugh—'

'And then you walked into my shop, and I felt something I thought was dead. And my first thought wasn't happiness. It was guilt.' He looked up at her, eyes red-rimmed. 'Because Sarah's only been gone four years, and what kind of man moves on that quickly? What kind of man looks at another woman and feels that pull when his wife is barely cold in the ground?'

'A human man,' Joanna said firmly. 'A man who's lonely and brave enough to admit it.'

'I don't feel brave. I feel terrified. Because if I let myself care about you—really care about you—and I lose you somehow, I don't think I could survive that again. I barely survived losing Sarah.'

They sat there, hands clasped, two broken people staring at each other across a chasm of fear.

'So, what do we do?' Joanna asked finally. 'Because I want this. I want you. But I'm terrified I'll mess it up, or you'll leave, or I'll wake up one day and realise this was all a dream.'

'And I want you,' Hugh said. 'But I'm terrified I'm betraying Sarah's memory, or that I'll compare you to her unfairly, or that Emma will get attached and then something will happen and she'll lose someone else she cares about.'

'We're a mess,' Joanna said with a watery laugh.

'A complete disaster,' Hugh agreed. 'But maybe that's all right. Maybe we can be disasters together.'

'How?'

Hugh thought for a moment. 'Friends first?' he suggested. 'We take it slow. Spend time together, get to know each other properly, but without the pressure of it being... more. Not yet. Not until we're both ready.'

'You'd be willing to do that?' Joanna asked. 'To wait?'

'I've waited four years,' Hugh said simply. 'I can wait a bit longer if it means doing this right. If it means not scaring you away.'

'I might still get scared. Might still panic and do stupid things.'

'Then you panic and do stupid things, and I'll try to understand.' His thumb traced circles on her palm, the same gesture from the café. 'And when I get scared—because I will, I promise you I will—you'll do the same for me. We'll be patient with each other.'

'Friends first,' Joanna repeated. The word felt both safe and insufficient. But it was a start. 'I can do friends.'

'Good.' Hugh smiled, and the warmth of it reached his eyes. 'Because I quite like you, Joanna Hartwell. And I'd like to keep you in my life, in whatever capacity you're comfortable with.'

They sat there a moment longer, hands still joined, and Joanna felt something in her chest settle. Not completely—the fear was still there, still whispering its warnings—but enough. Enough to take this next step.

'I should tell you,' she said, 'that I had a complete breakdown last night. Tried to pack my bag and leave. The cottage locked me in.'

Hugh's eyes widened. 'It what?'

'Locked the door. Wouldn't let me go. Kept me there until I'd cried myself out and realised I was being an idiot.' She laughed shakily. 'Mrs

Willoughby came this morning and helped me work through it. Told me I needed to stop living in what-ifs and start living in what-is. And what is, is that I want to stay here. I want to be part of this village. I want to give this—us—a chance.'

'The cottage locked you in,' Hugh repeated, still processing. 'Of course it did. That cottage has always been protective of the people who need it.'

'You don't think that's mad?'

'I think this village runs on its own rules. I stopped questioning the enchantment years ago.' He squeezed her hand. 'I'm happy you stayed. Very happy you didn't leave.'

'Me too.' And she meant it. 'Mrs Willoughby invited me to help plan the Imbolc celebration. Saturday at Rose Cottage. She said it was important that I come. Be part of things.'

'It is important,' Hugh said. 'Imbolc's special here. Marks the turn from winter to spring, from darkness to light. A good time for new beginnings.'

'New beginnings,' Joanna echoed. 'I like the sound of that.'

The shop door opened, and a young mother came in with a toddler, asking about picture books. Hugh stood reluctantly, squeezed Joanna's hand once more, and went to help.

Joanna watched him work. The way he crouched down to the toddler's level, let the child choose books, and chatted easily with the mother. He was good at this. Good with people, good with children, good at creating these small moments of connection.

She could see a future here. Could see herself in this shop, helping him, being part of his life. Being part of Emma's life. Scary thought. Wonderful thought.

After the mother left, Hugh came back. 'I should get back to work. But... would you like to stay? Just for a bit? You could sit and read if you wanted. Keep me company.'

'I'd like that,' Joanna said.

So, she did. She browsed the shelves, chose a novel—*84, Charing Cross Road*, about letters and books and long-distance friendship that became something more—and curled up in the armchair by the fire. Hugh worked around her, shelving and tidying, occasionally glancing over with a smile that made her heart do complicated things.

At one o'clock, Emma came in from

school—half day, apparently—and lit up when she saw Joanna.

'You're here!' She dropped her school bag and bounded over. 'Dad said you might not come back after—' She stopped, glanced at her father, whose ears had gone red. 'After Sunday. But you're here!'

'I'm here,' Joanna confirmed. 'Your dad and I have had a talk. We're all right.'

'Good.' Emma flopped down on the floor beside the armchair, proprietary and comfortable. 'Can I tell you about what we did in science today? It was brilliant. We're learning about photosynthesis and how plants make energy from light and—'

She launched into an enthusiastic explanation that involved a lot of hand gestures and scientific terms used with varying degrees of accuracy. Joanna listened, charmed despite herself, occasionally asking questions that made Emma's face light up even brighter.

Hugh watched them from behind the counter, and the expression on his face was slightly awed. As if he couldn't quite believe this was happening. That this woman was here in his shop, listening to his daughter ramble about chlorophyll, looking like she belonged.

At two o'clock, when Hugh suggested they close up early and maybe have tea in the flat upstairs, Joanna said yes without hesitation.

The flat was exactly as she remembered—cosy and cluttered and full of books and love. Emma made herself scarce after tea, disappearing to her room with homework, leaving Hugh and Joanna alone at the kitchen table.

'Thank you,' Hugh said quietly. 'For coming back. For giving me another chance.'

'Thank you for understanding why I ran.' Joanna wrapped her hands around her mug. 'And for being patient. For suggesting we take it slow.'

'Friends first,' Hugh said. 'But Joanna? I want you to know—I'm not going anywhere. I understand you being scared that I'll leave. But I won't. That's not who I am.'

'You can't promise that,' Joanna said. 'People die. People change. Things happen.'

'You're right. I can't promise forever.' Hugh reached across the table, found her hand. 'But I can promise today. And tomorrow. And every day after that, until one of us decides otherwise. Is that enough?'

Joanna thought about it. About living in what-is instead of what-if. About choosing, every day, to be brave.

'Yes,' she said finally. 'That's enough.'

##

When Joanna walked home that evening, the sky was clear for the first time in days. Stars were coming out, hard and bright in the winter dark. The temperature had dropped, but she barely felt it.

Hugh had walked her to the door, but this time when they said goodbye, there was no awkward almost-kiss. Just a hug—warm and careful and exactly right—and a promise to see her at the planning meeting on Saturday.

The cottage welcomed her home with warmth and light. The fire burned bright. In the conservatory, the flowers had multiplied again. The whole space was a riot of bloom now— snowdrops and crocuses and daffodils and those tiny blue flowers that smelled like hope.

And there, on the kitchen table where she definitely hadn't left it, was a small pot with a single green shoot just beginning to emerge from the soil. A note beside it in handwriting she didn't recognise:

Rosemary. For remembrance. But also, for new memories. Mrs W.

Joanna laughed and cried at the same time. Picked up the pot, carried it to the conservatory, and set it among the others. The shoot was perhaps an inch tall, impossibly green, reaching for the light.

Like her. Reaching for light after a long winter.

She sat in her chair and looked at all the impossible blooms surrounding her. Magic. Real, undeniable magic that said growth was possible even when everything suggested otherwise.

'Thank you,' she whispered to the cottage. 'For keeping me here. For not letting me run. For believing in me when I couldn't believe in myself.'

The warmth pulsed. The fire crackled. And very gently, very softly, something that might have been a sigh of contentment moved through the room.

Outside, stars sparkled brightly. The village settled into its Monday night. And in Hawthorn Cottage, Joanna sat surrounded by blooming flowers and thought about new beginnings.

She smiled. It was enough. For now, it was more than enough.

Chapter Eleven

Saturday at Rose Cottage was chaotic, wonderful, and Joanna sat there entranced.

Mrs Willoughby's sitting room was full of people—Vivian and Dimity, of course, and Margaret from the café. There were others Joanna hadn't met yet—the vicar, a young woman named Sarah Smith who wore jeans and a jumper instead of vestments. Two elderly sisters who ran the village shop. A man called Tom who managed the pub.

They were planning Imbolc, and everyone had opinions.

'Bonfire on the green, obviously,' Tom was saying. 'Same spot as always. I'll organise the wood.'

'And candles,' Vivian added. 'Hundreds of them. Wd did that where I grew up. We'll line the paths from everyone's cottages to the green. Create a river of light.'

'The children can make lanterns in school,' Sarah suggested. 'Paper ones, nothing too elaborate. They love being involved.'

'What about the blessings?' one of the elderly sisters asked. 'Do we do it like last year? Everyone speaks their hope for the year?'

The conversation flowed around Joanna. She sat with tea and biscuits, trying to follow along, overwhelmed by the easy camaraderie. Vivian and Dimity were newcomers as she was, and Sarah, the vicar, had only been there a year or so, but the others had known each other for years, decades in some cases. They had history. Belonged.

'Joanna, dear,' Mrs Willoughby said, pulling her into the conversation. 'Would you help with decorations? Margaret's brilliant at it, but she could use an extra pair of hands.'

'I don't know anything about—' Joanna started.

'Perfect,' Margaret interrupted smoothly. 'Fresh perspective. Come by Wednesday evening? We'll work on wreaths and garlands. Nothing complicated.'

And just like that, Joanna had been given a task and was a part of things.

The afternoon passed in a blur of planning and laughter. By the time she left at five o'clock, her head was spinning, but her heart felt lighter than it had in years.

She was part of something. Actually, properly part of something.

##

Sunday morning dawned clear and cold. Joanna went up the hill to watch the sunrise—her daily ritual now, as necessary as breathing—and when she came back, she found a note had been slipped under her door.

Lunch at ours today? 1 pm. Nothing fancy. Emma's excited. So am I. Hugh

Joanna held the note and smiled like an idiot. A long leisurely bath, and then she panicked about what to wear, changed three times, and finally settled on jeans and a soft green jumper that brought out her eyes. Not trying too hard. Casual. Friends having lunch. That's all it was.

Her hands were shaking when she knocked on the door of Hugh's flat at precisely one o'clock.

Emma answered, grinning. 'Dad said you'd come but I was worried you might get nervous and not show up. But you're here! Come in, come in.'

She dragged Joanna inside, took her coat, hung it carefully, and led her through to the kitchen, where Hugh was stirring something on the stove.

'Joanna.' He turned, and his smile could have lit the whole village. 'Right on time. I hope you like roast chicken. Emma insisted we make a proper Sunday lunch, which means I've been cooking since nine this morning.'

'You didn't have to go to all that trouble—'

'Yes, he did,' Emma interrupted. 'It's important. A first proper meal with a guest must be good. Gran said so.'

Hugh's ears went red. 'Emma, maybe don't mention everything Gran says.'

'Why not? She said you needed to make a good impression. That Joanna is special and you should treat her accordingly.' Emma looked at Joanna with that too-knowing expression. 'You are special, aren't you? Dad's been happier ever since he met you. He whistles now. He never whistled before.'

'Emma!' Hugh abandoned his stirring to steer his daughter towards the door. 'Why don't you set the table? And maybe give Joanna and me five minutes without you interrogating everyone?'

Emma giggled but went, leaving them alone in the small kitchen.

'Sorry,' Hugh said. 'She's been like this all week. Determined to make sure today goes perfectly.'

'It's sweet,' Joanna said. And it was. The idea that Emma cared, that she wanted this to work, made Joanna's chest warm. 'Can I help with anything?'

'Keep me company while I finish the gravy?' Hugh gestured to a stool by the counter. 'And tell me about the planning meeting yesterday. Emma said you were going.'

So, Joanna sat and talked while Hugh cooked. Told him about the chaos of the meeting, about being assigned to help Margaret with decorations, about feeling like she'd been swept up in something wonderful, if overwhelming.

Hugh listened and stirred and occasionally added ingredients to various pots, moving around the small kitchen with ease. He was good at this, Joanna realised. Cooking, creating, making a home for his daughter. He'd been doing it alone for four years, and he'd created something warm and safe and full of love.

'You're a good father,' she said without thinking.

Hugh paused mid-stir. 'Thank you. I try. Some days I'm better at it than others.'

'That's all any parent can do.'

'Were your parents good? Before the illness, I mean?'

Joanna thought about it. 'Yes. Not perfect, but good. Dad worked too much. Mum worried too much. But they loved me. Made me feel safe. That's what matters, isn't it? Making your children feel safe.'

'Emma's safe,' Hugh said quietly. 'But I worry she's not happy. Not completely. She misses having a mother. Having a woman in her life who can talk to her about things I don't understand.'

'She has your mother. And Mrs Willoughby.'

'She does. But it's not the same as...' He trailed off, then looked at Joanna directly. 'As having someone here. Someone who's part of our daily life.'

The weight of what he wasn't saying hung between them.

'Hugh—'

'I'm not asking for anything,' he said quickly. 'I promised we'd take this slow, and I meant it. I just want you to know that Emma likes you. Really likes you. And if this—us—does go somewhere eventually, she'd be happy about that.'

Joanna's throat went tight. 'I like her too. She's remarkable.'

'She is.' Hugh smiled, soft and proud. 'She's the best thing I ever did. Even on the hardest days, I look at her and think, well, at least I got this right.'

Emma appeared in the doorway. 'Are you two going to stand there being soppy, or are we eating? Because I'm starving and this table isn't going to admire itself.'

##

Lunch was perfect.

The food was excellent—roast chicken with crispy skin, fluffy Yorkshire puddings, roast potatoes that crunched outside and melted inside, vegetables that tasted like vegetables. Hugh had gone to enormous trouble, and it showed.

Emma talked nonstop about school, her

friends, and the book she was reading. She asked Joanna questions—what was her favourite book? What did she think of the village? Had the cottage done anything super magical yet? —and listened to the answers with genuine interest.

It felt like family. That was the terrifying, wonderful truth of it. Sitting at this table with Hugh and Emma, laughing and talking and passing dishes, felt like family.

After lunch, Emma insisted on showing Joanna her room. It was exactly what you'd expect from a twelve-year-old bookworm— shelves crammed with books, a reading corner with cushions and fairy lights, posters of fantasy landscapes on the walls.

'This was Mum's favourite,' Emma said, pulling a book from her shelf. *The Secret Garden*. 'She used to read it to me when I was little. Before she got too sick to read.'

Joanna's heart squeezed. 'It's a beautiful book.'

'You were reading it, weren't you? In the cottage? That's what Mrs Willoughby said.'

'I was trying to. I kept getting stuck.'

'But you're not stuck anymore?' Emma

asked.

'No. I found different books. Better books for where I am now.'

Emma nodded seriously. 'That's what Dad says. That we need different books for different times in our lives. And sometimes we need different people too.'

She set down *The Secret Garden* and looked at Joanna with an intensity that was unnerving. 'I asked the village to help Dad be happy again. Did you know that?'

'You did?'

'Last winter. I went up the hill—the same hill you go up for sunrise—and I stood there, and I asked. I said, please, please send someone who can make Dad smile again. Who can make him whistle and be happy like he used to be before Mum died.'

Emma's eyes were very bright. 'And then you came. So, I think maybe our enchanted village listened. I think maybe it sent you for us.'

Joanna couldn't speak. Couldn't breathe.

'I know you're scared,' Emma continued. 'Mrs Willoughby told me. She said you've been hurt before and you're worried about being hurt again. But Dad won't hurt you. He's the best person I know. And if you give him a chance, I think you could both be really happy.'

'Emma—' Joanna's voice cracked. 'I don't know what to say.'

'You don't have to say anything.' Emma hugged her suddenly, fiercely. 'Just don't give up on him. Please. He deserves to be happy. You both do.'

Joanna hugged her back, this brave, fierce, wonderful child, and felt tears slip down her cheeks.

When they went back downstairs, Hugh took one look at Joanna's face and pulled Emma aside for a whispered conversation that involved Emma looking sheepish and Hugh looking exasperated. But when he came back to Joanna, he just smiled and suggested they have tea.

They had tea. They talked. They laughed. And when it was time for Joanna to leave, Hugh offered to walk her home.

##

The walk was quiet. Not uncomfortable, just peaceful. The village was settling into Sunday evening, lights glowing in windows, the occasional sound of laughter or conversation drifting from the pub.

At Joanna's gate, they stopped. The cottage glowed behind them, warm and inviting. A light snow had started to fall, soft flakes that caught in Hugh's hair and made him look younger, softer.

'Thank you for coming today,' Hugh said. 'It meant a lot. To both of us.'

'Thank you for having me.' Joanna looked at her hands. 'Emma said something. Upstairs. About asking the village to send someone to make you happy.'

'She told you that?' Hugh groaned. 'I'm sorry. She shouldn't have—'

'No, I'm glad she did.' Joanna looked up at him. 'Because I think maybe it worked. The village, I mean. I think it sent me here for both of us. To help us both heal.'

Hugh was quiet for a long moment. Snow fell between them, soft and silent.

'I'm falling in love with you,' he said suddenly. 'I know we said friends first. I know we're taking it slow. But I need you to know that. What I'm feeling. Where this is going for me.'

Joanna's heart stopped. 'Hugh—'

'You don't have to say it back. You don't have to say anything. I just needed you to know.' He stepped closer, close enough that she could feel the warmth of him. 'Because I don't want there to be any confusion. Any doubt about what this is for me. I'm falling in love with you, Joanna. And I'm terrified. But I'm doing it anyway.'

'I'm terrified too,' Joanna whispered. 'But I'm falling too. I didn't think I could. I didn't think I'd ever feel this way again. But I am.'

'Yeah?'

'Yeah.'

They stood there, snow falling around them, looking at each other. And then Hugh asked, very softly, 'May I kiss you?'

Every instinct screamed at her to run. To pull away. To protect herself.

But Joanna thought about Emma asking the village for help. About the cottage that wouldn't let her leave. About flowers blooming in winter because magic said they could.

'Yes,' she said.

Hugh cupped her face in his hands—warm, careful, trembling slightly—and kissed her.

It was gentle. Tentative. Perfect. His lips were soft, the kiss chaste but full of promise. He tasted like tea and hope and all the good things Joanna had forgotten existed.

When they parted, she was smiling through tears.

'Would you like to come in?' she asked. 'I could make tea. And I'd like to show you something.'

Hugh's answering smile was incandescent. 'I'd love to.'

The cottage welcomed them both with a warmth that felt like approval.

Joanna led Hugh through to the conservatory, and he stopped dead in the doorway.

'Bloody hell,' he breathed.

Every surface bloomed. The amaryllis, the snowdrops, the crocuses, the daffodils, the tiny blue flowers, the rosemary Mrs Willoughby had brought. Impossible abundance in the middle of winter, all growing in defiance of nature and sense.

'This is...' Hugh moved into the space, turning in a slow circle. 'This is extraordinary.'

'Magic,' Joanna said simply. 'The cottage

has been doing this since I arrived. Helping me heal. Teaching me that growth is possible even when everything says it isn't.'

Hugh touched one of the amaryllis blooms reverently. 'I've lived here most of my life, and I still can't quite get my head around how the magic works. But this...' He looked at her. 'This is the cottage saying you're healing. That you're ready to bloom.'

'I think so.' Joanna moved to stand beside him. 'And I think maybe you're part of that. Part of my healing. Part of my bloom.'

Hugh turned to her, and the expression on his face was so full of love and hope and terrified joy that Joanna's breath caught.

'I should go,' he said, but he didn't move. 'It's late. Emma will wonder where I am.'

'You should go,' Joanna agreed, but she didn't want him to.

They stood there in the conservatory surrounded by impossible flowers, not quite touching but close enough to feel each other's warmth.

'Thursday,' Hugh said finally. 'Come for dinner. Just you and me. Emma's going to Gran's. I'll cook. We can talk. Just... be together.'

'I'd like that.'

He kissed her again, soft and sweet, and then forced himself to step back. 'I'm going now. Before I don't want to go at all.'

Joanna walked him to the door. Watched him cross the green, turning back twice to wave. When he disappeared from view, she closed the door and leaned against it, smiling like a lunatic.

In the conservatory, every flower seemed to lift towards the light.

And on the glass, written in condensation, two words: **About time.**

Joanna laughed until she cried, and the cottage hummed with contentment around her.

Chapter Twelve

The week passed in a blur of preparation and anticipation.

Wednesday, Joanna went to Margaret's—she had a studio space in the converted barn before the cafe—and learned to make wreaths from ivy and winter berries, garlands from evergreen branches. Her hands remembered skills she'd thought forgotten, muscle memory from helping her mother in the garden decades ago.

Margaret worked quickly, her long fingers deft with wire and ribbon. Dimity had joined them and was more enthusiastic than skilled, but her creations had character. The three of them worked and talked and laughed, and Joanna felt the threads of real friendship forming.

Thursday evening, she had dinner with Hugh.

He cooked *pasta carbonara*—and they ate at his small table with candles lit and music playing softly. They talked right through the meal. About books and dreams and the lives they'd lived before arriving at this moment. About Sarah, who Hugh spoke of with love but not crushing grief. About Marcus, who Joanna could finally mention without feeling like she'd been punched.

After dinner, they sat on Hugh's sofa with tea, and he held her hand, and they watched the snow fall outside the window. Hugh kissed her goodnight at the door—longer this time, deeper, full of promise—and Joanna walked home feeling like she was floating.

Friday, the whole village was buzzing with preparation.

Joanna helped wherever she was needed. Running errands for Mrs Willoughby. Collecting candles from the shop. Helping Tom stack wood for the bonfire. Small tasks, but each one made her feel more connected, more part of things.

The cottage seemed to feed off her happiness. Every morning brought new blooms in the conservatory. The fires burned brighter. Even the weather seemed to respond—the snow stopped falling, the sky cleared, temperatures rose just enough that standing outside for the evening celebration wouldn't be torture.

Saturday morning, Joanna woke before dawn for her hill walk and found Hugh waiting at her gate.

'Thought I'd join you,' he said with a smile. 'If that's all right.'

They climbed the hill together, his hand finding hers as they walked. At the top, among the pines, they watched the sun rise together— gold and pink and orange flooding across the Cotswolds, painting everything beautiful.

'This is my favourite time of each day,' Joanna said softly. 'When the world is waking up. When everything feels within reach.'

'Like new beginnings,' Hugh said.

'Yes. Like that.'

He kissed her as the sun cleared the horizon.

This is happiness, Joanna thought.

February first arrived clear and cold.

Imbolc. The turning point. The moment when winter acknowledged that spring was coming, that light would return, that hope was real.

Joanna spent the afternoon helping with

final preparations. Candles placed in paper bags weighted with sand, lining every path from cottage to the village green. Wreaths hung on doors. Garlands were strung between lampposts. The bonfire was built high and ready, waiting for darkness.

At five o'clock, she went home to change and dug out her favourite dress—deep green wool, simple but elegant. She brushed her hair until it shone, put on the pearl earrings her mother had given her a lifetime ago.

In the mirror, she barely recognised herself. Who was this woman with eyes that sparkled and cheeks that glowed? This woman looked happy, alive and like someone who belonged. Joanna smiled at her reflection and walked into the conservatory.

It was a riot of bloom. Every pot, every surface, covered in flowers. And there, in the centre of it all, a new amaryllis had pushed up overnight. Its bud was enormous, splitting already to reveal petals of the deepest crimson.

'Thank you,' Joanna whispered to the cottage. 'For everything. For keeping me here. For helping me heal. For giving me a chance at my life.'

The warmth pulsed, strong and steady as a heartbeat.

At dusk, the village gathered.

Joanna emerged from Hawthorn Cottage to find candles already lit, creating rivers of light from every cottage to the green. People were walking slowly, reverently, following the light. She joined the flow, and Margaret from the café fell into step beside her.

'Beautiful evening for it,' Margaret said. 'Perfect weather. The village is pleased.'

'The village is pleased?' Joanna asked.

'Our village always knows when something important is happening. When someone's healing. When someone's found their place.' Margaret smiled. 'You've found yours, haven't you?'

'I think so,' Joanna said. 'Yes. I think I have.'

The green was transformed. Hundreds of candles flickered in the gathering darkness. The bonfire stood ready, and Tom was there with a torch, waiting for the right moment. The church bells began to ring—not a call to service, just a celebration of sound, marking the turning of the season.

People gathered in a large circle around the unlit bonfire. Joanna found herself between Mrs Willoughby and Vivian, with Dimity on Vivian's other side. Across the circle, she could see Hugh with Emma, both of them scanning the crowd. When Hugh's eyes found hers, he smiled, and Emma waved frantically.

Sarah, the vicar, stepped forward.

'Friends,' she said, her voice carrying clearly in the cold air. 'We gather tonight to mark Imbolc, the festival of returning light. Winter is not over—we know this. There will be more cold days, more dark nights. But tonight, we acknowledge that the tide has turned. Spring is coming. Hope is real.'

She gestured to the unlit bonfire. 'Tonight, we light this fire as a symbol of all the ways we carry light—in our hearts, in our communities, in the small acts of kindness that sustain us through winter.'

Tom stepped forward and touched his torch to the bonfire.

It caught immediately, flames roaring up into the dark sky. Heat rolled out in waves, pushing back the cold. The circle of people moved closer instinctively, drawn to the warmth and light.

'And now,' Sarah continued, 'we share our hopes for the year ahead. What light do you want to bring into the world? What do you hope will bloom in your life as we move towards spring?'

She spoke first. 'I hope for continued community. For connection. For this village to keep being a place where people heal and find themselves.'

Mrs Willoughby went next. 'I hope for love. For all of us. In whatever form it takes. Love is the greatest magic there is.'

Around the circle, people spoke their hopes. For health, for happiness, for good harvests and successful businesses and children who thrived. For creative projects and mended relationships, and the courage to try new things.

Hugh's turn came. He looked across the fire directly at Joanna.

'For courage to love again,' he said clearly. 'And for the wisdom to do it right this time.'

Emma, beside him, squeezed his hand and grinned.

The circle continued. Vivian spoke of

gratitude for second chances. Dimity spoke of love. Margaret spoke of purpose.

And then it was Joanna's turn.

Everyone was looking at her. The entire village gathered in firelight, waiting to hear what she hoped for.

She could feel the gravity of the moment. This was more than just speaking words into the cold air. This was claiming her place. Declaring her intention. Choosing her future.

'For trust,' Joanna said, her voice shaking but clear. 'And for home. For believing that I'm allowed to have good things. That I'm allowed to stay. That I'm allowed to bloom, even after the longest winter.'

The circle was silent for a moment. Then Mrs Willoughby reached over and squeezed her hand. Dimity did the same from the other side. And around the circle, people nodded, smiled, accepted her words as truth.

The moment passed. The next person spoke. But Joanna stood there with tears on her cheeks and warmth in her chest and the absolute certainty that she'd just done something irrevocable.

She'd claimed this. All of it. The village, the

cottage, the magic, Hugh, Emma, the life she was building here.

She'd chosen to bloom.

After the circle finished, the gathering became a celebration.

Someone produced instruments—a fiddle, a guitar, a bodhrán. Music filled the air, lively and joyful. People danced or stood talking in small groups or roasted marshmallows over the edges of the bonfire. Children ran about with sparklers, writing their names in light.

Hugh found Joanna in the crowd.

'Hi,' he said, slightly breathless.

'Hi yourself.'

He took her hand and pulled her away from the centre of things, towards the edge of the green where the light from the bonfire was softer, the shadows deeper.

'I meant what I said,' he told her. 'About finding the courage to love again. That was about you. You know that, right?'

'I know.' Joanna stepped closer, not caring who might see. 'And I meant what I said, too. About trust. About home. This is home now, Hugh. You're part of that home.'

His eyes went very bright. 'Yeah?'

'Yeah.'

He kissed her there in the firelight, with the village celebrating around them and music playing and her new life spreading out in all directions like light.

When they parted, Emma was there with a knowing grin.

'About time,' she said. 'I've been waiting for you two to stop being silly about each other.'

'Emma!' Hugh started, but she just laughed.

'Come on. Mrs Willoughby's made hot chocolate. And we're supposed to walk back to your cottage together—all three of us. That's what people do on Imbolc. Walk each other home to make sure everyone has light to follow.'

She grabbed both their hands and towed them back into the celebration.

The three of them walked to Hawthorn Cottage together as the celebration wound down.

Other groups were doing the same—small processions following the candlelit paths from green to door, making sure no one went home alone, everyone had light and company.

At Joanna's gate, they stopped. The cottage glowed from within, warm and welcoming. Like it had been waiting.

'Would you like to come in?' Joanna asked. 'Both of you? I could make tea. We could sit in the conservatory. I'd like you to see it properly, Emma. See what the cottage has done.'

Emma looked at her father, hopeful. Hugh nodded.

Inside, the cottage wrapped them all in warmth. The fire roared in greeting. Emma gasped when she saw the conservatory—the impossible abundance of bloom, the riot of colour and life and magic.

'It's beautiful,' she breathed. 'It's the most beautiful thing I've ever seen.'

She moved among the flowers carefully, reverently, while Hugh and Joanna stood in the doorway watching.

'She's right,' Hugh said quietly. 'It is beautiful. You're beautiful. All of this—what you've built here, who you're becoming—it's extraordinary.'

'I'm just healing,' Joanna said. 'Same as everyone else.'

'Maybe. But you're letting us be part of it. Letting us in. That takes courage.'

Emma had found the newest amaryllis—the one with the enormous crimson bud. 'Dad, look. It's about to bloom. Like, tonight probably.'

She was right. As they watched, the bud trembled. A petal unfurled, then another. Slowly, impossibly, the flower opened before their eyes.

Deep red, almost burgundy, with a throat of pure white. Enormous and dramatic and utterly, impossibly alive.

'Magic,' Emma whispered.

'Magic,' Joanna agreed.

They stood together—the three of them—and watched the amaryllis bloom. Watched winter become spring, as darkness became light, and hope became real.

Outside, the last of the Imbolc celebrants were finding their way home. The bonfire burned down to embers. The candles guttered one by one. The village settled into February, into the slow turn towards spring, into the promise that light always, always returned.

And in Hawthorn Cottage, surrounded by

impossible flowers and the people who'd helped her remember how to hope, Joanna felt something she hadn't felt in ten years.

Joy.

Pure, uncomplicated, terrifying, wonderful joy.

January had given its gift. The long winter was ending. And Joanna—broken, frightened, brave Joanna—was finally, finally ready to bloom.

Much later, after Hugh and Emma had gone home with promises to see her tomorrow, after the cottage had settled into contented silence, Joanna sat in her chair in the conservatory and looked at the amaryllis that had bloomed before her eyes.

On the glass, in condensation that formed as she watched, words appeared: **Welcome home.**

Joanna smiled and touched the glass. 'Thank you. For everything. For not giving up on me. For believing I could bloom when I didn't believe it myself.'

The warmth pulsed—strong, steady, sure.

Outside, stars wheeled overhead. The village slept. The millstream burbled past. And on the hill above it all, winter snow began to melt, revealing the first green shoots of spring beneath.

Hawthorn Cottage had healed another wounded soul; it had taken someone broken and helped them become whole. Had woven its gentle magic until hope became real and winter became spring and endings became beginnings.

And tomorrow, and the day after that, and all the days that followed, Joanna would wake in this enchanted village and choose, again and again, to be brave.

To trust.

To love.

To bloom.

It was January's joy.

THE END

March Magic… coming March

Ten years of marriage. Ten years of hope, disappointment, and the slow, silent drift that comes when every month brings fresh heartbreak. Sophie and Daniel Ashford thought a fresh start in the Cotswolds might save

them—a sabbatical, a break from the constant
medical appointments and whispered apologies.
Just six months in Violet Cottage to remember
why they fell in love.
But Violet Cottage has other plans.
A tender story of marriage, grief, and the
courage it takes to start again with the person
you thought you'd lost.

Available for print pre-order in Annie's
store:
https://annieseatonstore.ecwid.com/March-
Magic-Pre-order-March-p803861302

Also by Annie Seaton

Daughters of the Darling
From Across the Sea
Over the River
By the Billabong
Beneath Still Waters
Under Darling Skies

A Bec Whitfield Mystery
Bowen River
Shadows on the Shore
Storm Season
Dark Waters

Enchanted Village Series
A Magic Christmas
January Joy
March Magic
Mayday Magic
Midsummer Magic
Harvest Magic

The Happy Outback Hotel (2026)
Outback Strangers
Outback Secrets
Outback Dreams
Outback Hearts
Outback Spirit
Outback Promise

Outback Horizon
Outback Silence
Outback Whispers
Outback Flame

Duckinwilla Days
Coming Home
Secrets and Surprises
Wishes and Whispers
Chasing Dreams
New Beginnings
All Together Now

Home to the Outback
Lucy
Angie
Jemima
Isabella

Porter Sisters Series
Kakadu Sunset
Daintree
Diamond Sky
Hidden Valley
Larapinta
Kakadu Dawn

Others
Whitsunday Dawn
Undara
Osprey Reef
East of Alice

ANNIE SEATON

One Summer in Tuscany
Four Seasons Short and Sweet
Follow the Sun
Ten Days in Paradise
Deadly Secrets
Adventures in Time
Silver Valley Witch
The Emerald Necklace
A Clever Christmas
Christmas with the Boss
Her Christmas Star
The Emerald Necklace

The Augathella Girls Series
Outback Roads
Outback Sky
Outback Escape
Outback Wind
Outback Dawn
Outback Moonlight
Outback Dust
Outback Hope
Boxed Sets
Augathella Girls 1-4
Augathella Girls 5-8
Augathella Short and Sweet Series
An Augathella Surprise
An Augathella Baby
An Augathella Spring
An Augathella Christmas
An Augathella Wedding

An Augathella Easter
An Augathella Masquerade Ball
Boxed Set
Augathella Short and Sweet 1-3
Augathella Short and Sweet 1-4

Sunshine Coast Series
Waiting for Ana
The Trouble with Jack
Healing His Heart
Sunshine Coast Boxed Set

The Richards Brothers Series
The Trouble with Paradise
Marry in Haste
Outback Sunrise
Richards Brothers Boxed Set

Bondi Beach Love Series
Beach House
Beach Music
Beach Walk
Beach Dreams
The House on the Hill Boxed Set

Second Chance Bay Series
Her Outback Playboy
Her Outback Protector
Her Outback Haven
Her Outback Paradise
The McDougalls of Second Chance Bay Boxed Set

Love Across Time Series
Come Back to Me
Follow Me
Finding Home
The Threads that Bind
Love Across Time 1-4 Boxed Set
Bindarra Creek
Worth the Wait
Full Circle
Secrets of River Cottage
A Clever Christmas
A Place to Belong
Hearts in Harmony

Awards

2024: Finalist – Romantic suspense category, RUBY award for *From Across the Sea.*

2023: Winner - Long contemporary novel category, RUBY award for *Larapinta.*

2023*:* Finalist - Australian Romance Readers Awards for *Kakadu Dawn,* the sixth and final book in the Porter Sisters series.

2018 and 2020: Finalist - for the NZ KORU Award.

2017: Winner - Best Established Author of the Year 2017 AUSROM

2017: Winner - Author of the Year 2014 AUSROM
 Best Established Author, Ausrom Readers' Choice.

2016, 2017, 2018, 2019: Longlisted - Sisters in Crime Davitt Awards

2016: Finalist - Book of the Year, Long Romance, RWA Ruby Awards for *Kakadu Sunset*

2015: Winner - Best Established Author of the Year AUSROM